COUGARS

THE PACK RULES #5

MICHELE BARDSLEY

❀ Created with Vellum

ALL ABOUT THAT SASS

PART I

1

Gareth Harper sat at the scarred wooden table in a shifter bar he'd been partial to since he'd been in the area. The werewolf family that owned the place welcomed all who entered. In here, he felt safe. He'd been alone since his half-brother, Craig, had banished him from the werecougar colony. Gareth was considered a pariah and no werecat within the Harper territory would give him the time of day. *Outcast.* The word tasted bitter on his tongue. But the alternative was death, and he wanted to live—even if that meant a wanderer existence.

Gareth looked around the bar. The worn but comfortable furniture, the yeasty smell of beer, the easy smiles of both staff and customers—he took it all in. He needed to move on soon, but his reluctance to give up the unexpected solace he'd found in the bar stalled him.

"Gareth," said a female voice, filled with warmth. He knew immediately who'd said his name. He looked up and saw the smiling face of Debra. The barmaid checked on him every now and again, and it felt good to be cared for ... even if it was only for a little while.

"How are you?" he asked.

"I'm right as rain," she said, sliding the coffee in front of him. "You're the only furball in here who prefers coffee to alcohol. This is a bar, you know."

He grinned. "I like being different."

"That's good," said Debra, her gaze sliding across the room. "Because I think that young lady wants different."

Gareth followed Debra's unabashed stare.

Whoa. His heart tripled its beat—the result of an undeniable attraction to the woman sitting at a corner table near the windows.

His body strained toward hers as though they were magnetically connected. Every molecule in his being screamed, *"Her. Her. Her. Now. Now. Now."*

"Well, then," said Debra. "My work is done." She patted his shoulder and left him alone to drool at the gorgeous female within catching distance.

Gareth knew by her scent that she was a human. He never thought a human female would trigger his mating urges. The very idea baffled him. In this territory, many outcasts made their homes in the forests and the small towns that comprised the area. Either the lovely lady was passing through, or she lived somewhere nearby. Not for the first time, he felt the urge to settle down, put down roots. But why? And with who? Making home with someone was a pipe dream.

Okay, moron. Get. A. Grip. He looked around the dark bar with its neon drink signs and empty stools. He tried to find something to take his mind—and libido—off the brunette. It took less than thirty seconds for his gaze to return to the woman.

His cock got hard. Rod-of-steel hard. And the fantasies his mind spun about the woman made his body rigid with desire. Gareth gave up pretense and stared openly at her. She was curvaceous, with the face of an angel. Her cheekbones were rosy, her lips fully kissable, her nose turned up just a smidge at the end. There was shimmering beauty about her. Abstract and untouchable. Goddess-like.

Lust heated his blood, thrummed through his balls and did more damage to his cock. Her flawless skin required little make-up. Her hair was the color of milk chocolate and her eyes sparkling amber. She was medium height, luscious beyond reason, and dressed for the cold weather in boots, jeans, sweater, and a leather jacket. She sipped her coffee and read something apparently riveting on her tablet.

She lifted her gaze and caught him in the act of checking her out. *Schmuck! Get out of here before you do something really stupid.* Like tell her, "Oh, I think you might be my mate. By the way, I'm a shifter. Let's get busy."

His stomach clenched. No. No way. He'd been banished from the territory where his family lived. His brother had made sure his banishment had been public, humiliating, and permanent. Gareth had been the only threat to Craig's claim to alpha. His older brother had always been a soulless dick.

Gareth slid out of the booth, put on his coat and put a $5 on the table to cover his untouched coffee. As he reached to push open the front door, he found long, pale fingers wrapped around his wrist. Startled, he looked into the gaze of the woman who had tilted his world on its axis.

"Hello," she said. Her eyes sparkled with humor and intelligence and — oh shit — attraction. His gaze drifted down to the hand on his sleeve. Her nails were neatly trimmed and coated with clear polish.

"I'm sorry," she said, her smile revealing a dimple near her right cheek. "I didn't realize you were mute."

"I'm not," he said.

"Ah. My name's Angela Ross. And you are?" She had a Southern twang, which was delightfully softened by her honeyed voice.

He cleared his throat and managed to say, "Gareth Harper."

Angela leaned close, and the floral scent of her perfume drifted around him. "Would you be up for a little experiment, Gareth?" she asked. "I've never been with a werecougar."

Shocked, he stared at her. How had she known about his dual nature? "What are you talking about?"

"Oh, sugar, you don't have to lie to me. I know you're not a shifter like those portrayed in movies." She spoke in the same tone one would use to discuss the weather. Gareth drew in her scent. Definitely human. And pure delicious female. He tended to forget that some humans knew about shifters. Members of his colony kept themselves under wraps. Too many assholes had tried hunting them—and gotten dead for their efforts.

But here, in this territory, it was different.

"Angela." A tall man joined them, his mossy green gaze assessing Gareth. His eyes held curiosity, not hostility. Still, when the fellow wrapped his arm around Angela in a clear show of possession, Gareth wanted to bare his fangs and rip off the guy's limbs. He tamped down the urge. The man had silvery blond hair tied back in a leather thong. His skin was pale, almost luminescent. He was dressed in the same casual way as the woman—jeans, sweater, boots, and jacket. He was lean—had a swimmer's build. He had no underlying scent. In fact, he had no heartbeat, no breath.

Vampire.

Gareth had never met one.

The man extended his hand and Gareth took it, held it in a tight grip and pumped. "My name is Thomas Moore."

"Gareth."

He looked at Angela. "He's the one?"

She nodded. "I felt the pull, like you said."

"And did you?" asked Thomas.

Gareth blinked. "Did I what?"

"Feel the mating urge with Angela?"

Gareth's mouth dropped open. "Why would you want that? Isn't she yours?"

"I don't belong to anybody except myself," said Angela. "I choose my life." She winked at Gareth. "And my partners."

Thomas leaned over and kissed the top of Angela's head. "Isn't she magnificent?"

Gareth nodded numbly. Had he fallen into an alternate universe? He'd never imagined finding a mate, much less one who was already in a relationship.

"We consulted a psychic," said Angela. "She said we would find the one we needed if we went to where no one rules. We figured out that part—but finding the right place. Whew. This was the fourth one we've tried."

"Yeah. That makes total sense. Not crazy at all. Um, I should probably go," he managed, his voice hoarse.

"We have a cabin with a toasty bed," offered Angela. Gareth suppressed the shudder of delight that accompanied Angela's hand squeezing his shoulder. Then her slim fingers sifted through Gareth's hair. Gareth swallowed his sigh of happiness. "You know you wanna."

Yes! agreed his cock, *you really do wanna.* Occasional lovers had been only sips of water in the desert of his love life. Still, he hesitated. There was an undercurrent of emotion here that he didn't understand. It rippled between the three of them—a powerful, connective energy.

"Please." Angela's blue eyes were filled with naughty promises. "I won't bite."

Gareth leaned forward and bared his canines, growling. "I can't make the same claim, sweetheart."

2

Gareth drove his sedan about three feet from the bumper of the Land Rover navigating the rough dirt road. Large trees rose on either side, sentinels of the thick forest beyond. It appeared the promise of sex was enough motivation to throw caution to the wind. For all he knew, the vampire planned to feast on him, and the woman, the one who caused the mating urge to roar inside him was merely bait.

Well, hell. What did he have to lose? He was alone. Abandoned by the Harpers, what few remained, and unhappy. Less unhappy than he'd been under the thumb of his older brother, but still.

They turned onto a gravel road, and soon came upon a cozy cabin. Billowing gray clouds covered the moon, hiding the forest in shadows. None of the windows offered illumination. Not even the porch light was on. Gareth wondered if it was because the vampire liked the dark or because they wanted people to believe the place was unoccupied.

He stepped out of the car. His superior eyesight took in the well-worn logs that comprised the cabin, the repaired planks on the porch, and well-tended area around the home. It hardly seemed like the place where a vampire and a human might murder a werecougar. The sharp scent of pine filled his nostrils. The winter wind chased dead leaves across the gravel then rattled the bare limbs of the trees lurking near the house.

"Lovely, isn't it?" asked Angela in a delighted voice as she took Gareth's hand and led him toward the steps. "I fell in love with it the first time Thomas brought me here. It's a perfect love nest."

Gareth caught Angela's smoldering glance. His heart skipped a beat. He wasn't sure what he'd gotten himself into ... a human female and her vampire lover? Anticipation thrummed through him as a simple, primal need overrode common sense and logic.

The mating urge roared inside him, insistent—no more than that. Bordering on feral.

He wanted whatever happened next.

As Gareth waited on his companions, he studied the huge four-poster bed, its wispy gold curtains pulled back to reveal the plush comforter and mountain of silk-covered pillows. The bedroom had its own hearth and a fire burned brightly.

Obviously Thomas and Angela spent a lot of time in here. Tonight, they would make room for him in their bed. He couldn't help but wonder, just a little, if it were possible for them to make room for him in their lives. Even if he and Angela were mates, that didn't mean she wanted him on a permanent basis. Especially since she already had a man. He sighed. Gareth didn't belong anywhere anymore. He tried not to think about the werecougars he'd once called family.

"What's done is done," said Thomas.

The vampire had sidled behind him so silently Gareth's cougar senses hadn't picked up his movements. "You're reading my mind," he accused softly.

"You're wondering about us. About our motives."

"I'm wondering about my own motives." Gareth gestured around the room. "She's a human—and yet, I feel the mating pull. How is that possible? Mating is not reserved for shifters. But it's rare for shifters to mate with humans."

Thomas cocked a brow. "Is it?"

"Well, for werecougars. We're ... discouraged from mating with humans." He paused. "You said a psychic told you to find me?"

"Psychic. Ah. Some vampires have better developed abilities. The one we consulted in New York pointed us in this direction."

"Why did you consult a psychic vampire in the first place?"

"Boys," said Angela.

The men turned, and Gareth saw that Angela wore nothing but a smile.

Her skin was golden in the firelight. Her thick curves made his mouth water. Her hair swung like a chocolate waterfall over her shoulders. She winked. "What do you think, sugar?"

The growl that issued from his throat surprised them both. Her expression told him that she wasn't scared, just intrigued. He scooped her into his arms and strode to the bed, with Thomas following.

Gareth made short work of his clothes and noted that Thomas did the same. Gareth wasn't against having an *ménage a trios*. But he damned sure planned to be the one who worshipped Angela first. He wanted her so badly he shook with hot, urgent need. He crawled onto the bed and covered her. His cock nestled against her warm sex; her tight curls pressed softly against his length. She wrapped her legs around him and kissed him. Her tongue was small and soft. She teased without trying to possess.

He was drowning in her scent, her touch, her beauty. She felt so good. He lightly bit her collarbone, licking his way to her breasts. They were large and soft, tipped in pink. He sucked on one delicious peak, lightly nipping her.

She moaned. That breathy sound went right through him. He tormented her other breast, just so she'd do it again. He squeezed and licked and bit until she issued moan after moan.

"Gareth," she whispered. "My beautiful Gareth."

She shifted, adjusting herself so that his shaft teased her entrance.

Gareth hesitated.

"What's wrong, sugar?" Her blue eyes were luminous, filled with desire and need and... something else. It wasn't that being with Angela, and by default Thomas, felt wrong. But there was something else, too, and he couldn't pin it down.

Angela kissed him and reached for his cock. They touched each other, lust-driven desperation guiding their hands and mouths. Gareth trembled as he and Angela made love. He was immersed in a thousand wonderful sensations.

"Let me fuck you," said Gareth, his voice thick with lust.

Angela pressed against his chest, offering him more of her delicious kisses, her damp sex rubbing his cock.

They rolled onto their side, allowing Thomas to press

himself against Angela. He stroked her flesh and kissed her neck, as Gareth took her mouth and pressed against her.

"I need you," whispered Angela. She took Gareth's cock inside her.

Gareth groaned, trying to remember to breathe. Lovemaking had never been this intense before.

Angela kissed him, squeezing him as Gareth slowly deepened his penetration until his hard length filled Angela's sex. While Thomas touched and kissed Angela from her backside, Gareth started a slow rhythm. She moaned again and again as he took her, gifting him with those delightful mewling sounds.

"Now," she demanded. "Both of you ... claim me."

Sudden, intense pleasure cascaded through Gareth, a drugging joy that made him want to give her the mate bite. *This is right. This is the way it should be.*

Thomas sank his fangs into Angela's shoulder. Gareth's teeth extended, his teeth sharp and dangerous, and he bit Angela at the top of her breast. She cried out, both ecstasy and pain in the sounds.

"Oh, yes," whispered Angela. "Come inside me, Gareth. Please."

The orgasm shattered him. It was like a bomb going off. Big, bright, overwhelming. He clutched Angela and rode the wave of it, his seed jetting inside her. Her lips found his, her tongue thrusting into his mouth hard and fast as she came, her wet sex milking his cock with hard, slick pulses.

For a long, tender moment, they held each other. Angela was the first to move. She kissed Thomas and then moved off the bed. Thomas followed, but Gareth was too sated to attempt movement. He laid there, eyes closed and happily exhausted, until he heard Angela scream.

3

Gareth saw Thomas and Angela standing in front of the hearth. He leapt from the bed and got in-between them before the vampire could blink.

"What are you doing?" asked Thomas.

"Protecting her."

"Oh, silly! He's not hurting me." She did a little dance. "You did it, Gareth. We knew you were the one!"

Confusion rioted through him. He turned to her. "What did I do?"

"You gave her what I could not," said Thomas, grinning broadly. "A child."

Gareth's eyes widened. "How could you possibly know that she's pregnant?"

"I'm a vampire," he said. "I know."

"It's why I wouldn't let him turn me," said Angela. "Because I wanted a baby. I wanted us to have a baby." She kissed Gareth and did another jig. "And now I'm gonna have one!"

Stunned, Gareth slumped into one of the wingbacks positioned in front of the fireplace. This was what he couldn't pinpoint—the need Thomas and Angela had for him. Not just satiation of lust, but another purpose; to give them a child. How could he have believed she was his mate?

He looked at the wound on her breast. It bled, but she didn't seem to notice. He'd claimed her. They were mated. Mates needed each other.

At least, that's what he'd been led to believe. Now, he was not only mated to a human female—who was already claimed by a vampire, but he was soon to be a father. *What have I done?*

If Craig ever got wind of Gareth's situation, he was a dead man. Angela and their child would never be safe.

"It's not easy being a werecougar," he said bitterly. "Being different in the werecat world means you're weak. Unwelcome."

"As a member of this family, any differences are welcome," said Angela. "Our baby will be fine. You'll see."

Gareth stared at her. "I will?"

"Of course. You're with us now." She pointed to her bite mark. "Remember?"

"My brother rules the Midwest werecat colony. He won't like this. He's dangerous."

"You're not part of that community, right?" asked Thomas.

"I was banished, so no, the colony is not my home anymore. And never will be again."

"You were meant for us," said Angela. "And we were meant for you."

He wanted to believe her. But he couldn't. It was too surreal. "We don't know anything about each other. Or if we're compatible or if we'll even like each other tomorrow."

"That's the stupidest thing I've ever heard. We're together now, and that's that." Angela patted her tummy.

"Our baby will be loved so well. Just like we love each other. Oh, look!" She hurried to the double windows, unlatched them, and swung them open. "It's snowing!"

She stood there, naked and shivering, enjoying the falling snowflakes. Gareth and Thomas shared a look, mutual joy for their mate, and then they, too, went to the windows and stood with her in the swirling snow, each man shielding her with his body. Gareth felt the ache he'd carried with him for so long disappear, filled by the affection and acceptance of two strangers, who were now his family.

Gareth realized that somehow, some way, he'd found exactly where he belonged.

PART II

4

Eight Months Later...

Cyn Salais peered through the thick branches of the pine tree that hid her presence. She was twenty feet up clinging to the trunk, her feet lightly resting on a limb not quite as thick as her arm. Below her was the cozy cabin that belonged to her target, the vampire Thomas Moore.

The wind kicked up, the first volley from the threatening storm. The branches rattled and the top of the tree swayed. Cyn readjusted her grip, inhaling the sharp sting of pine. Here in this mid-western cesspit, June meant it was unbearably hot and humid. Sweat popped out on her forehead and dribbled down her temples. Usually she wore a jacket to hide her Walther PPK snug in its shoulder holster, but she couldn't add another layer to her long-sleeved knit shirt, jeans, and boots—all black. Her knives were hidden in their usual spots.

The unseasonable clothing, including the gloves, was necessary for her concealment. Her skin was too pale, more a result of her declining health than lack of sunshine.

Cyn continued to study the cabin for what seemed like the fiftieth time in two days. She'd counted three: Thomas, a werecougar, and a very pregnant human woman.

When Cyn had had decided to take Eliza DuChamp's offer of eternal life, she'd observed the vampires lounging around the opulent New York penthouse with humans sitting next to them like dogs on leashes. Cyn's stomach clenched. She couldn't imagine being a bloodsucker's pet. It made her sick, the way that bitch Eliza kept nibbling the neck of her female slave. The poor girl was naked, and pale from blood loss. And the look in her eyes...

Cyn shuddered.

She returned her attention to the cabin. Her paranormal education had only begun a month ago, but even she knew the werecougar prowling the front porch was bigger than most. She watched as the massive animal padded through the open front door of the cabin. She'd seen werewolves, but this was her first shapeshifting kitty. She always knew the world was a weird place. Still, the idea humans shared the planet with supernatural creatures was more weird than she ever believed possible.

"Fuck," she muttered. She'd had bad odds before, but dealing with a werecougar, a vampire, and a pregnant female? Even if she managed to complete her objective and live, she still had to worry about whether or not Eliza would keep the bargain.

Eliza was pissed off at her ex-lover for ditching her for a human woman. Not only had he dissed her by abandoning their relationship, he'd gone and committed the ultimate sin: he was creating a family. The woman's baby couldn't be his, of course. Vampires couldn't breathe much less breed. If she had to guess, the werecougar and the human created the child. And her observations over the last two days had given her the impression that Thomas and the shapeshifter were both in love with the woman. She had two fierce protectors. Cyn had to take them both out.

Not an easy task.

Hell, maybe even an impossible one.

But what did she have to lose?

She needed to survive, and that meant pulling off this job for Eliza. All she had to do was kill a few people and Eliza would change her into a vampire. It wasn't an ideal situation. But it was better than death. She was only twenty-eight, damn it. The only way for Cyn to live was to die and re-awaken as a bloodsucker. Either that, or wait for her heart to give out. Fucking cardiac tumor. The malignant mass was lodged in her heart like a living bullet—killing her day by day.

Cyn hoped that taking out Thomas was where her obligation ended, though she suspected she'd made a deal with the devil. Eliza was not the beneficent type. Either she'd sent Cyn to her death because she loved to cause pain and misery, or she wanted to further utilize Cyn's skills as an assassin. Screw that. No way was she gonna spend her new eternity offing the powerful vampire's enemies. After she was changed, all she had to do was keep out of Eliza's range. That scary bitch was cra-azy.

Cyn studied the area surrounding the cabin. Thickly wooded, embedded at the top of a hill with a steep drive, the place was isolated. And it wasn't exactly well protected, which would usually make it perfect for a hit. But that damned werecougar—getting him out of the way would be a pain in the ass.

The wind was getting stronger, and in the distance, thunder cracked. The tree shook, harder this time, and Cyn's booted feet scraped against the limb.

It was time to put up or shut up.

As she climbed down, she solidified her plan of action. She'd wait for the storm, which would make good cover. She'd have to draw out the shapeshifter and get him alone. After dispatching him, she would sneak into the cabin and kill Thomas. She'd figure out something for the female. It wasn't that Cyn was opposed to killing women. Putting down any living thing because death was the better option, well, *that* made her stomach cramp. Hey, even she'd cried at the end of "Old Yeller." But she wouldn't kill a mother and her child, even though Eliza had demanded it as part of their deal.

Jesus. She'd thought humans were the biggest assholes on the planet. Then she'd met Eliza and entered a whole new world of cruelty.

Cyn was an expert at hand-to-hand combat and knife fights; her father had made sure of that. Still, her Walther PPK with its suppressor was a far better tool for murder.

Unless the target was a vampire.

Yeah, silver hurt vampires, but not even silver bullets would kill them instantly. She'd learned about a rare poison mixed with silver flakes supposedly fatal to vamps, but she didn't know how to get hold of it or how it was administered. She preferred more foolproof methods. Poison had too many variables, not least of which was the quality of the death. She killed people, yeah. Honestly, most of her targets deserved killing. But that didn't mean she made them suffer.

Her policy? Quick. Clean. Done.

Cutting off a vampire's head wasn't even a surety. If the head came in contact with the neck, it could suture back together. Yeah. That info had freaked her. But whack through the neck with a pure silver blade... then the fanged one was toast.

She'd been given the short sword forged from pure silver, save for its hilt that was made from Red Quebrancho —one of the hardest woods in the world. The short sword was the only insurance she had for incapacitating paranormal beings. Granted, shifters reacted more violently to the substance, but it took a lot of silver to kill them. And silver had to stay in contact with the shifter for a long time.

At least that's what her sources had told her. She'd never killed vampires or shifters, so she didn't have firsthand knowledge of their weaknesses; much less the death knells of either species. She wasn't exactly feeling her best, not with her ticker failing, and going into a new situation with this much risk ... well, it was no wonder she felt foreboding lining her guts like lead.

She stopped lollygagging on the last limb, and jumped to the ground. Her arsenal included her usual weaponry, along with the short sword, which hung in its scabbard on her left hip. It wasn't heavy, unlike the burden of her debt to Eliza.

According to the rumors in the paranormal community, the last time a bloodsucker betrayed Eliza, the dude had been dismembered and his head had been stuck on a pike and kept in the vampire bitch's bedroom.

Yuck.

It was one thing to kill, and another to bask in the aftermath of murder. That was the difference between Cyn and a serial killer. That, and the money. She never did a hit for free. And never, ever for jollies. Some people were just sick.

Cyn leaned against the tree, and took a moment to gather her thoughts. Immediately, her mind opened the door to that night in New Orleans. She'd been in her hotel room, pacing and crying, and Eliza had just ... appeared.

She still didn't know how Eliza had found her. New

Orleans had been one of Cyn's bases of operation, and that was where she'd gotten the diagnosis. Then boom! Eliza showed up and spouted off ridiculous crap like "I'm a vampire."

Then she'd proven it. Eliza had opened the door into a whole new world—a world in which Cyn could live. And she had badly wanted to live.

After a month of hanging out with vampires, even with the occasional atrocities, she hadn't been turned off enough by the lifestyle to chuck it as an option. Just because other vampires acted like they owned the afterlife didn't mean she had to do the same. There were ways to ingest blood that didn't include killing innocents. She'd spent a good deal of her time putting bullets into skulls, but she'd chosen her jobs, and could say that most of her targets had been real dickheads.

So thirty days with the vamps, and she'd figured she knew enough about them and shifters to get the job done. It wasn't like she had forever to plan and execute. The doc hadn't been able to pinpoint exactly how long she had to keep breathing. *Three months, if you're lucky,* he'd said. *I'm sorry*.

Now, that meant two months. Maybe. Probably less.

The evening before she left, Eliza gave her the silver sword in its scabbard. "Bring this back to me along with proof of Thomas' death," she said, "and you'll get your reward."

The word "reward" had the same ominous resonance as "death," and Cyn had thought about rejecting Eliza's sword outright. Still, she tamped down the impulse. If her father had taught her nothing else, it was to think before she acted. But Eliza had seen Cyn's hesitation.

"You think you can kill a vampire with mere bullets?"

Eliza's voice had gone soft, seductive. "Who do you think cornered the silver market? Shifters. They control silver because it's the one substance that can harm them. It doesn't stop peddlers from selling fakes. Sometimes, there's actual silver in them, but that hardly matters. Only pure silver rounds will affect shifters ... or vampires."

Damn. Eliza knew that Cyn had purchased silver bullets. Or thought she had. "You want me to owe you a favor for the sword," she'd said flatly. "I'm already taking out your enemy."

"In exchange for eternal life. Now, I'm doing another favor for you." She smiled, revealing sharp fangs. "And you owe me one in return," she said. "That's how you survive in this world. Remember that." She'd flickered like an image on a bad film reel, and disappeared.

Cyn had packed the sword.

If Cyn could kill Thomas with her bare hands or any of her weapons, she would've told Eliza to shove that sword right up her undead ass. God. She didn't want to owe Eliza anymore than she already did. If the silver blade was the only way to take out a vampire or a shifter, then Cyn had no choice.

Oh, what was she worried about? If Cyn died doing this gig it would be no worse than dying because of a heart tumor. Going out quick would be a mercy. Better than waiting for her heart to give out.

Cyn inhaled a cleansing breath then blew it out slowly. After a minute of deep breathing and focusing on the first task of the job, she used the trees for cover and headed toward the cabin.

5

"Maybe we should shift back into cougars," said Aris. "Sitting here naked is kinda stupid."

"It was your idea to go human for a while." Kane leaned against another tree, taking in everything around them. "We agreed no clothes until the mission is over. We've destroyed enough garments on this trip."

"I wish I'd brought more underwear. I'm down to one pair of boxers."

Kane laughed, and it was good to hear the sound. Not that Kane was ever the life of the party. He didn't find much humor in life; in fact, Aris was one of the few people who could get the man to crack a smile.

"We'll hit Wal-Mart after we're done here, okay?"

"Are you sure there's not a Neiman Marcus nearby?"

Kane rolled his eyes. "For a warrior, you worry too much about your wardrobe."

"When you look good, you feel good."

"Unfortunately for you, this town is too small to have a high-end clothing stores. They have a Wal-Mart. Deal."

"Ugh."

They'd been roaming the area in their cougar forms waiting for the storm to let loose. Aris had gotten bored, and shifted into his human form. After Kane shifted, too, and had bitched about him breaking cover, he decided that maybe it would be all right to hang out naked in the forest. Kane wouldn't admit it, but Aris's more relaxed attitude occasionally rubbed off on him. Besides, they were alone out here except for some woodland rodents, and nobody in the cabin had a clue that warriors were waiting for an opportunity to kill the werecougar inside.

Aris re-positioned himself against the wide base of the oak tree. The bark made his skin itch. From their vantage point, they could see the back of the cabin. The brewing storm was rumbling louder now, and he could smell the change in the air. It would rain soon, and then, they would sneak inside and do their duty as guardians.

Aris felt sick about the whole thing.

Killing Gareth Harper sucked ass.

"Craig will be pissed when we tell 'em that we tore out his brother's throat."

"He did not forbid us," said Kane, though his voice was edged in worry. "And no matter what Craig says about Gareth, he should be killed honorably."

The fact that Kane was going against the spirit of their leader's orders obviously bothered him. But at the end of the day, Kane stuck by his own principles, even if they clashed with the powers-that-be. It was a quality that Aris admired, when it wasn't irritating the fuck out of him.

Kane was ten years older, thirty-four to his twenty-four. In human years. Werecougar years were another matter entirely. The man was 6'6" and built like an ancient oak. Hard-fought battles had robbed the warrior of his ability to breed. With Aris, a genetic anomaly had taken away his fertility. One of the reasons Kane and Aris had become such good friends, aside from the fact that Kane had trained Aris as a guardian, was that neither one could have children. Unfortunately, it also meant that mating was out of the question. No werecougar in her prime wanted infertile mates. For all intents and purposes, Kane and Aris were pariahs, even though they still lived within Craig's territory and had pledged their loyalty to him.

Fat lot of good it did us.

Craig cared nothing for their plight—until Gareth's location had become known. To gain their cooperation he offered the one thing they'd both been denied: a mate. One to share, but so what? He and Kane had shared before. The woman in question had already bore children who were now adults, and had been widowed a year earlier. She'd agreed to take both of their mating bites and let them claim her. In a way, she was much like them. Since she was no longer useful to the colony—at least in their leader's eyes—she was easy to sacrifice.

So were they.

That's why Craig had sent them to kill his younger brother. If they failed and died, it wouldn't be a loss. If they succeeded, then great, no valued warriors would have to be sent to finish the job.

He didn't like Craig. Neither did Kane.

Yet, here they were.

Aris sighed. Kane had been secretive lately, and he wasn't exactly a sharer of his feelings. Aris didn't go around spouting poetry or reading self-help books, but he also wasn't as internal as Kane. Something big was bothering the older man and Aris knew from experience there was no getting it out of him.

Aris picked up a rock and tossed it from hand to hand.

He was getting antsy again. They'd checked out the place last night, figured out how to get in, and then gone over the plan a billion times. Booooring.

"Gareth is already banned. Why bother killing him now?" he asked idly.

"If he hadn't put his seed into a human, he'd still be waking up tomorrow morning."

"I don't get it. Humans have had shifter babies before."

"Craig's blood is royal. So is his brother's. I don't think our esteemed leader likes the idea that his precious family line would be diluted by human blood. And the fact that Gareth has aligned himself with a vampire doesn't help, either."

Aris dropped the pebble he'd been messing with. He wanted to hit something: the tree, the ground, the smug face of Craig Harper. He'd invited them to his lux home in the middle of nofuckingwhere and assigned them the task of killing Gareth. He hated how Craig put politics and nonsensical dictates before the welfare of his people. Or so it seemed to Aris.

But not to Kane. Kane, who followed the regs every single day of his life. Kane was consistent. He was steady. He was thoughtful. He *planned*.

Aris... not so much.

Aris glanced at Kane, who was staring at him and frowning. Well, he could frown all he wanted. He had doubts about this course of action, too.

After giving up his friends and his status, Gareth had found happiness. He was gonna be a father. Aris thought about Gareth's child growing in his mate's womb. She was nearly at term. Craig had only recently become aware of his brother's location and the human's pregnancy, and he'd acted quickly. Hybrid breeding was an intolerable sin against the royals. In Craig's view, Gareth had committed treason, which was an automatic death sentence. He would die, and so would the woman carrying his abomination. And the vampire.

Craig had made it clear that all three were to be killed.

Aris's stomach squeezed with dread. He didn't want to kill Gareth. And he sure as hell didn't want to hurt a mother-to-be. "Kane ... what right do we have to kill Gareth and his mate?"

"If we want a mate, we must do this."

"But what if we took a human female?"

"Aris..."

Aris knew that tone. It was Kane's you'll-understand-when-you're-older Dad voice. Argh! "Don't patronize me!" He pushed away from the tree and started pacing. He wanted to be heard, and he was tired of Kane ignoring his opinions. "What's duty without honor? Killing Gareth feels wrong."

Kane remained still, his massive strength leashed by his ever-present patience. Aris wished he were capable of that kind of control. But he was impulsive, and he knew it. He hated to wait around, not when he could take action and get things going. Kane could hold his emotions in check. Aris blurted his out. He couldn't keep shit to himself.

"Leave Gareth to his life," he said. "Let's just go home."

"If we don't abide by Craig's ruling, we won't have a home," responded Kane. "Do you ever think before you act?"

"Maybe I don't think enough," said Aris, "but you think too much."

Kane's mouth curled into a rare smile. Then his eyes went wide. A pained gasp escaped as he staggered sideways.

What the —

A woman stood there, silent, practically a shadow despite her height.

She moved fast. She yanked the silver sword from Kane's back, and tossed something at Aris' head.

He caught the throwing star, but the seconds-long distraction cost him. By the time he'd crossed the distance, she was already moving. "You little bitch!"

She kicked him in the solar plexus. Hard. His lungs nearly collapsed and he bent over, dropping the star. She kneed him in the face before scooping up the star. Aris fell, gasping. She plunged the sword into Aris' kidney, acidic agony burst inside him.

He roared in pain.

The attacker jerked out the sword and stalked toward the older shifter. Kane had collapsed to his knees. He was too much of a warrior to scream, but the silver was doing its job. He was shaking, obviously in excruciating pain.

She aimed the blade at Kane's carotid artery.

Aris snarled, leaping to his feet, and dove at her.

She whirled away, sheathing the sword. Then she turned and ran, not away into the woods where he could scent and catch her, but to the nearest tree. She grabbed the lowest branch and swung up, catching another limb with gloved hands and using it to climb further into the tree. He heard her thrashing, the scrape of her boots against the trunk, and then she jumped into a nearby oak.

And she kept going.

Even as fury pounded through him, he was damned impressed by her skills. She wouldn't get away, no matter how fancy her moves. And when he caught her, she was getting a throat full of his teeth.

Unfortunately, that wouldn't be tonight. Not with Kane injured.

Heart hammering, both pissed and worried, Aris knelt next to his friend, his mentor. "C'mon. I'll get you to safety."

"Get. Her."

"I'm not leaving you." Aris would take Kane back to the rental car. It was a clusterfuck now. Why had she attacked them? Was she protecting Gareth? That didn't make any sense. Gareth was more than capable of kicking ass, and he'd never give the job of protecting himself and his mate to someone else.

What the fuck was going on here?

Kane gripped his arms and used Aris's strength to help him sit up. "Can't. Leave." He struggled to take breaths and Aris felt panic well. Kane sucked in a breath. "I'm healing. Go... g-get her."

"I'll kill her."

"No!" Kane shook his head. His teeth were chattering and his lips turning blue. It felt like a hundred degrees out here even with the storm brewing, so it was bad that Kane had taken a chill. "Just restrain her."

Aris wanted to argue. Instead, he zipped his lips. Kane was in pain, his body trying to heal the effects of the silver. She'd jabbed three times, deeply. The wounds on Kane's back were blackened — one of the results of silver touching shifter skin.

"I'll stay here. Need t-to heal."

"Dude. You look like shit." He didn't want to leave Kane. What if his body didn't detox the silver?

"Been through this before." He gulped in air. "Can't let her go. Might warn our targets."

"All right, already." Aris could give two shits about whether or not Gareth knew they were there. Maybe the royal could talk some sense into Kane. But right now, he just wanted Kane to feel better because Aris was seriously freaking out.

He helped Kane to the same tree where he'd been sitting earlier. Kane leaned against the trunk. He was taking deep breaths, and he'd stopped shaking. He really was healing. Okay, that was good.

"You're w-wasting time."

"I'll get her."

"Alive," reminded Kane. "Got it?"

Aris nodded. When he caught the woman, he'd keep her alive, but that didn't mean he wouldn't punish her for what she'd done. Still breathing constituted alive, right?

You can run, he thought as he stood up and began the change from human to cougar, *but you can't hide*.

6

Cyn paused top of a pine tree, and sucked in steadying breaths. Her heart hammered, skipping its beats, letting her know it was gonna fail her ... maybe right now.

The sneak attack on the werecougars hadn't gone well. Watching the men shift from werecougar to human was both beautiful and frightening. Both men were the epitome of strength and grace. She'd severely underestimated the shifters. If they'd met in another circumstances... She shook off her thoughts. Freaking paranormals. Those dagger wounds would've killed a human. Not to mention she would've been able to deliver the killing blow.

The other guy had moved fast. He'd snatched the throwing star right out of the air and if he hadn't been distracted by his partner's injuries, he might've actually gotten her. She'd seen the animal glinting in his eyes. She'd seen her death in those eyes, too.

What to do? Complete the assignment? Or bail?

There was no way to tell if she could get to the house,

kill Thomas and crew, and get out before the kitties caught up to her. Still...

Cyn's heartbeat was still erratic, and panic was threatening. She took calming breaths, and imagined that the organ was steadily beating, that it was healthy and whole. After a long moment, the rate stabilized. It was getting harder and harder to use that technique. Her heart had stopped listening to her Jedi mind tricks.

If she didn't complete her assignment she was dead. Eliza would send someone to finish her. Even if she did manage to kill Thomas, Cyn's heart could fail before she could get back to the court and go through the change.

What am I doing?

She chewed her bottom lip as she looked over her shoulder. She could turn back, go to the cabin, and complete her assignment. Inside was death for the vampire and redemption for her. Only she wasn't sure she wanted it anymore. Squatting in a tree, listening to the thunder roar as the air thickened with rainy intent, she face the other direction. She could walk away—from this gig, from Eliza, from eternal life. WWDD? What would Dad do?

Her father had been black ops, part of a small group of agents who were in the deepest of the deep within the CIA. He'd demonstrated how she should protect herself, trained her to kill quickly and efficiently, and helped her shape perspective not only about the job but also about her own life. He showed her that mercy wasn't a weakness. Jose Salais had also explained one of the most important rules in the world of assassins: know when to get out.

"Okay, Dad," she said, blowing out a breath. "I'm out."

The choice was clear now. The choice she should've made when the cardiologist gave her the bad news. *I'm not meant to be here anymore.*

She'd go somewhere with a beach, gorgeous men in Speedos, and fruity umbrella-laden drinks. Definitely someplace where sunshine was so plentiful, no vampire would even think of hanging out there. She'd soak in every moment until her heart gave out.

She'd wasted enough time, damn it.

She had to make it all the way down the hilly drive, a few blocks east, and to the bar. It seemed a hundred miles away, especially if the werecougars were tracking her.

Maybe they weren't. She'd injured the big dude badly. And his younger friend, angry as he was at her, seemed like the loyal type. He wouldn't leave his partner to chase after her.

At least she hoped so.

She'd stick to the trees until she got to the road. Then she'd run for it. Despite the doc's advice about exercising, she'd kept up her workouts. Her heart had survived the weight training and runs up till now, right?

Rain burst from the thick morass of gray clouds, and she grinned. That would definitely help mask her scent and the noise of moving through the forest. She climbed out on the branch, gauged the distance, and leapt.

Aris returned to the tree where Kane still rested, and shifted into his human form. "Fucking rain."

"You're not a kitten," rasped Kane. "You know how to find prey during storms."

"Yeah, if they're on the ground. She's in the goddamned trees." Despite Kane's protests, Aris helped the older man to his feet. "She's some kind of ninja gymnast."

Kane chuckled. "We need to find her."

"We're going to the rental car and back to the hotel," said Aris. He was mad. Mad that some chick had gotten the drop on them. Mad that Kane had gotten hurt. Mad that he hadn't been able to find Miss Stab-and-Run. "Don't give me any shit about it."

They'd wrapped their clothes in plastic, but still had to get dressed in the pouring rain. They were soaked to the skin by the time they'd made it to the road.

"Why'd we park at here?" Kane asked. He'd kept up the hurried pace Aris set, but it was obvious he was still dragging ass. "It feels like a thousand miles away."

"Can you make it, grandpa?" asked Aris.

Kane's dark eyebrows winged upward. "Grandpa?"

"The way you're moving? Yeah. You kinda remind me of a little gray-haired old man." He glanced over. "You want me to go get you a walker? Maybe a cane?"

"Fuck you." Kane started to run.

Aris caught up easily. He knew that Kane was still in pain; he was running to prove he could. Good. Aris needed his friend strong because they were going to find ninja girl ... and deliver some payback.

When they jogged into the parking lot, Aris grabbed the car keys from Kane and slid into the driver's seat. It said a lot about how his mentor was feeling that he didn't even offer a token protest. The storm had definitely cooled things off, but the mix of heat and wet was making him itch for a shower and a beer.

"Do you think she contacted Gareth?" he asked, half-hoping she had so that they could drop this insane mission.

"We won't know her purpose for being there, or for trying to kill us, until we catch her." Kane blew out a sigh and turned to Aris.

"There's something I must tell you."

Here was the moment when Kane finally told him about the big something he'd been hiding—bearing the burden on his own. Aris's stomach cramped. He had a feeling he wasn't gonna like the news.

"We won't be mating with the widow Craig promised us."

"What? That rat bastard! What the hell—"

"This has nothing to do with Craig. He's unaware that we are not sticking to the bargain."

"We aren't? What the fuck, Kane?"

"Leona came to me."

Aris felt like he'd been punched. "The mumbo jumbo lady? She's crazy."

"She's a well respected shaman, and she has the sight. She told me you and I would find our mate when we went to kill the outcast."

"You knew? Even before Craig asked us to take on this stupid mission?" Aris paused. "You mean we are both meant for the same woman?"

7

Kane nodded, his gaze unsure. That was so weird Aris could barely fathom it. Kane usually just did whatever, and Aris followed along because he'd learned Kane was nearly always right. He trusted him without question. Then a few pieces of this whole strange puzzle clicked into place. "We were never going to kill Gareth, were we?"

"No. We were waiting for her. I just never expected her to try and kill us. "

No wonder he'd been so moody. The motherfucker felt guilty. "We're supposed to be partners. You shouldn't have made this decision without me. You should've told me. Damn it, Kane! We could've come up with a plan together."

"I know that now. We are equals, and I should treat you as such."

Aris was caught between being really pissed off, and utterly amazed. He turned in the seat and looked at Kane. "Had you *asked* me, I would've agreed to this."

"I'm sorry. I should've consulted you."

Aris's eyebrows rose nearly to his hairline. "Did you just apologize? You never apologize."

Kane struggled to respond. Finally, he offered, "I'm sorry. Really damned sorry."

"Shut up, you pussy."

Kane grinned.

"She's human," Aris pointed out unnecessarily. Kane had lost his mind. He wanted to mate with the chick who'd tried to kill them.

"So what?"

"Good Goddess! You want to track down our would-be murderer. Talk her into mating with both of us. Then go on the run forever because Craig's gonna feel homicidal after we betray him."

Kane nodded. "Yeah. That about sums it up."

Aris stared at him for so long, he made Kane uncomfortable enough to look away. His gaze flickered toward the window; his eyes widened.

"It's her," Kane whispered. "She's unlocking that green car a few spaces away." He peered out the window. "It's a Prius."

"Prius? One of those hybrid cars? Our killer has an eco-conscience?"

"Apparently." Kane looked at Aris. "We'll go out on the left, circle our car from the back, and surprise her."

Aris was all in. He hoped they were able to freak her the way she'd freaked them. He was a trained warrior, a fucking werecat, and it chapped his fur that a human female had gotten the drop on him. Frankly, if Kane hadn't been so caught up in his own emotional angst, he would've never let Aris distract him. Aris was awesome in battle so long as someone else took the lead, and Kane was a born leader.

Kane quietly popped open the door and slid out to the

ground, crouching as he used the SUV for cover. Aris followed, shutting the door. He met Kane at the bumper. They peered around. Three spaces down he saw the back end of the Prius. Only one car was parked between theirs and hers. It was a rusted Toyota, and not exactly big enough to hide them.

"What's she doing?"

Kane shot an annoyed look over his shoulder. "Putting on lipstick? Shining her silver daggers? How the fuck do I know?"

Aris rolled his eyes. "She should've taken off by now."

"Let's take advantage of it. We'll go in fast," said Kane. "I'll take the back. You take the front."

"She has a gun," warned Aris. "Probably silver bullets, too. And those goddamned blades."

"Noted." Kane sent Aris one last look. "Go!"

They took off. Kane ran behind the parked cars, and Aris rounded the Toyota, and skidded to the side of the Prius. The woman looked up at him, her mouth rounded in an "O" of surprise.

Naturally the doors were locked, so he bashed in the window. Glass shattered; his knuckles bloodied. He bared his teeth and growled. "Remember me?"

He reached in and unlocked the passenger side door. He moved to restrain her, but she wasn't trying to fight. He realized then something was wrong. Her face was gray. Her shaking hand clenched a prescription bottle.

"Aris!" Kane waited on the driver's side, his gaze impatient. Aris unlocked the door. Kane threw it open, reached in and pulled out the woman.

"What the hell is wrong with her?" asked Aris. This wasn't the way he'd expected for things to go down.

"I don't know." Kane pried the bottle from her hand and

read the label. Then he opened the cap and poured out a pill, sticking it between the woman's blue lips.

"Swallow," commanded Kane.

Her eyes went wide, rolling into the back of her head, and she convulsed once before going limp.

"That went well." Aris exited the car. "Is she dead?" He squatted on the other side of her and looked down, more surprised than worried. He hadn't forgotten she'd stabbed Kane and tried to impale him with a throwing star.

"Unconscious." Kane pried her mouth open and looked inside. "She managed to swallow the meds before she passed out."

"What now?"

"I'll put her in the SUV. You follow me back to the motel in the Prius."

"Why do I have to drive the Prius?"

Kane slanted him a look, but obviously decided the insult was too easy. He scooped up the girl and stood. "Get going, princess. Your sparkly green chariot awaits."

"Oh, fuck you."

8

Cyn awoke in a cave. What the hell? She felt strange, as if she were as substantive as shadows. Lounging by the fire pit were two cougars. One was big with shining gold fur, his dark eyes serious. The other had more white under his maw and his blue eyes were filled with mischief.

"They are yours," intoned an elderly female voice. It bounced off the craggy walls, straight into Cyn. Of course, she thought, I've been waiting for them.

The cougars got up and padded to her, one settling on each side of her. She lay with them, their soft fur tickling her naked flesh. She sank her hands into their luxurious coats. Her body rippled with sensual awareness.

Then each werecat gave a low, possessive growl, and licked her breasts.

"No," said Cyn. But they wouldn't be denied. The bigger one put his paw on her rib cage, and his companion followed suit.

Their broad, flat tongues tortured her breasts and nipples, making her tingle and ache.

Then she felt a tongue lick up her neck, to her ear, and a male voice said, "You're beautiful."

The werecougar was no more. Deliciously naked, the man's long, thick cock pressed against her thigh. His skin was the color of coffee with too much cream, and his tousled hair was black, as dark as his eyes.

"Hmm," said another male voice. "She tastes good, too."

This man, as corded with muscle as his friend, had the mischievous gaze of the smaller cat.

They took turns kissing her, their hands stroking every inch of her heated skin. And when one of them parted the slick inner folds of her pussy and stroked her clit, she moaned, and closed her eyes, and fell down, down, down...

~

"She survived," said a male voice, laden with sarcasm. "Yay."

Cyn pried open her eyes and had barely realized she was laying in the middle of a comfortable bed when she felt the mattress dip. She looked at the man sitting inches from her.

Fuck.

Cyn sucked in a shaky breath, and tried to slough off the miasma. "W-what happened?"

Yep. It was Hottie No. 1, the dude she'd tried to off. Her gaze flicked beyond him, to the guy leaning against the hotel room wall. His glare clearly indicated that he wished she'd explode. Yeah. He'd been the one attempting to track her. Hard to do when she was in the trees with the battering rain washing away her scent and masking her movements.

She smirked.

He pushed himself off the wall and stalked toward the bed.

"Relax, Aris."

Blue Eyes stopped, pivoted, and threw himself into a chair tucked into the corner of the room. He crossed his arms and glared at her some more. Nice.

"I'm Kane," said the man on the bed. "That's Aris." He studied her face. "We've got you. So cooperate."

"Or what?" Her voice sounded like rusty hinges. She tried to clear her throat, but the effort hurt. It felt like she'd swallowed a whole bag of cotton balls. Kane helped her to a sitting position and handed her a glass of water. It had the metallic taste of tap water. What? She didn't rate the ten-dollar bottled water? Still, she sucked down every drop. She toyed with the idea of slamming the glass against Kane's gorgeous head, but he plucked it out of her hands. Oh well, it wasn't like she could take them both down, not without weapons or in her weakened state.

Her traitorous heart beat steadily, not revealing its weakness. She'd been so close to getting on that beach. Now, she was gonna bite it in a hotel room. Heh. Bite it. Yeah, that was probably the literal interpretation of how she would breathe her last. What a way to end an otherwise stellar career.

"Thanks for the water." Her voice sounded normal, and she was feeling a smidge better. She looked down at herself, and her lips quirked. "And thanks for leaving on my bra and panties. I usually like to get to know my killers personally before going nude."

"You must be naked a lot," Aris said.

"No one's ever gotten the drop on me," she replied. "How about you?"

Kane chuckled, but it wasn't a nice sound. "You have the distinction of nearly besting two of the best werecougar guardians on this side of the Mississippi."

"If you do say so yourself."

"If it's true, it's not bragging," said the one called Aris.

Warrior werecats? Like the regular kind weren't badass enough. Wow. She sure could pick 'em.

Cyn sat up. Then she heard a rattle and something flew at her. She snatched the prescription bottle out of mid-air.

"What are they for?" asked Kane.

She stared at the label. Kane had given her the meds. He could've let her die, right there in the parking lot, and gotten his revenge. Why had he saved her? So he could kill her himself? If that was true, the dude's ego was way too big. She didn't get that vibe, though. What a waste of energy and resources. If a target died of a heart attack instead of a bullet headache so much the better.

She put the bottle on the nightstand. She was gonna die. What was the point of lying? "My name is Cyn. And before you ask, yeah, it's just Cyn. I'm twenty-eight. I've been a paid assassin, trained by my father, since I was seventeen. I'm dying. My heart's giving out, and I have maybe a couple months to live."

Both men exchanged a look. "Why were you at the residence of Gareth Harper?" asked Kane.

"Who the hell is Gareth Harper?" Cyn remembered the huge cougar checking the cabin's perimeter. She realized these guys hadn't been protecting the house at all. "Harper's the kitty. And you're not his friends, are you?"

Kane and Aris exchanged a glance. Then Kane said, "As a matter of fact, we are."

"Yeah. Sure." She shrugged. "I was there to take out Thomas Moore. His ex-girlfriend offered to change me if I killed him." She laughed, a bitter sound. "I wanted to live so bad." Sighing, she flopped back to the bed and stared up at the ceiling. "I wonder if that's what people think right before I put a bullet in their skulls. *I want to live.*"

"These people you killed," said Kane. "They deserved it?"

"Yeah. I choose my jobs carefully. All but this one." She turned her head. Kane was leaning against the wall now, his eyes on her. Aris's baby blues glittered with an emotion she couldn't define, but at least he looked less hostile. "So what's going on here, boys? 'Cause if you ain't gonna do me, then I have a beach chair and a mai tai with my name on it."

"Do you?" asked Kane with a sexy growl that made her scramble off the other side of the bed.

"Whoa there. Do. As in kill." Cyn had nowhere to go. She'd fight like a rabid bitch, but she knew her odds. They'd get what they wanted. She planted her hands on her hips and glared at them. Her heart skipped a beat then started fluttering like a trapped bird.

"I prefer the alternative definition," said Kane.

"You saved me so you could fuck me?" Her voice was a mixture of outrage and astonishment.

"Not quite." He hadn't moved, but she got the distinct impression that both he and Aris were fully prepared to leap from their positions. The energy of the room had changed. Tension was so thick that she was nearly breathing it.

"I swear to God if you touch me, at least one of you will die."

9

Both men's expressions turned to shock.

"You think we would force you?" Aris rose from the chair and stared at her. The fury was back, although for a different reason.

"You kidnapped me and stole my clothes."

Aris settled down. "Well, there's that."

Kane's gaze hadn't left Cyn's face, and he was making her nervous.

"I'm a prisoner," she pointed out, feeling unaccountably defensive. "You could've let me die, but you didn't. And apparently, you're not trying to kill me. What am I supposed to think?"

"We have a proposal," said Kane.

Aris snorted and plopped back into the chair. He crossed his arms and took a supreme interest in the ceiling.

"I'm listening." Cyn stayed where she was, between the wall and the king-sized bed. Wary didn't begin to cover how she was feeling. What the hell did these guys want?

"We were sent by our leader to kill Gareth."

"Your so-called friend?"

"Gareth was our leader's half-brother. He was banned from the colony."

"Too much competition for that asshole," said Aris.

"Gareth impregnated a human female. That's a sin too great to forgive for our leader."

"Vampires can't have kids," she said slowly. The woman was pregnant. And if Kane was right, the woman wasn't the vampire's pet. She was in a threesome with a werecat and a vampire. Hmm. Maybe she was a little crazy. Well, she would've been safe from Cyn. No kids. Ever. And that included pregnant women.

It appeared these shifters didn't have the same policy. Her gaze flicked over Kane, who looked as stoic as a statue. She didn't understand werecougar politics any better than she did the machinations of vampires. "So, you're gonna kill Gareth for knocking up a girl? That's harsh."

"She's a human," said Aris. "Apparently not fit to carry our spawn." Aris sounded disgusted with the whole enterprise. Her respect for him went up a notch. Then she realized what he was implying.

"You're supposed to kill her, too?"

"She carries a half-werecougar," said Kane. He didn't sound too sure about this part of the plan.

"And I thought the vampires were fucked up."

"We're not doing it." Kane's sudden, fierce declaration made Aris's gaze swing toward him.

"Our true purpose has been accomplished," said Kane to his buddy. "We found her."

Cyn's eyebrows went up, but the men weren't paying attention to her. Aris stood up and put his hand on Kane's arm. "What about Craig? He's gonna be pissed."

"Screw Craig. We'll go to Gareth and tell him the truth. We'll have to if we hope to save Cyn."

Save me? Cougar say what now?

"We'll be in hiding forever." Aris's expression wavered between relief and worry. "And so will Gareth and his family. With the half-breed alive, Craig will never stop looking for them."

"Well, I'm not killing the vampire, either," she interjected. "In case you were wondering."

Both men turned to her. Cyn realized she should've kept her trap shut. Even though she'd been plotting to kill Thomas, she'd never met the guy. She had no investment in his life or the lives of those he loved.

Cyn thought about the vampire, the werecat, the human, and their baby. She felt a catch in her throat. She'd never been in love. In brief relationships, sure, and maybe a crush or two as a teenager before her first kill, but she'd never had the opportunity to fall in stars-in-the-eyes love. Just another regret she added to the "wish I had done this" list.

"If we've decided everyone's going to live," she said, "then I'd like my clothes." She paused. "And my gun."

"You haven't heard our proposal." Kane looked at her, his expression suddenly thoughtful. "You'd already decided not to kill your target. That's why you left after you attacked us."

"I decided it was time to listen to fate. I'd rather go have some fun before the ol' ticker gives out." She tapped her wrist as if it held a watch. "And now, you're wasting what little time I have left. So ... clothes?"

"I like you better without them on," Kane said. Aris leaned against the wall and studied her.

Once again, the atmosphere in the room shifted. The tension was there, but it was definitely the lustful kind. Cyn felt vulnerable. And though she'd spent every waking second being decisive, she found herself waffling. Were they offering a night in their bed? Was she insane for even thinking about how awesome fucking two werecougars would be?

Aris's gaze flicked to Cyn. "I want her," he admitted. "I want the one who can make us better warriors, men, cougars. She won't put up with shit. She's fast and strong." He grunted. "And, you know, pretty."

"Yeah. Um ... hello? I have no idea what you're talking about, but I'm not afraid to walk outta this hotel in my bra."

"You said you'd decided to follow fate," said Kane. "So have we. You don't have to die, Cyn. We can make you a werecougar."

"Not us, per se," added Aris. "Only royals have the changing bite."

She laughed. "You're going to ask Gareth, the dude you were sent to kill to save the girl who's supposed to off his whole family? That'll be good." Cyn looked at Kane, at the desire glittering in his eyes. Apprehension warred with hope. "What's the price of this gift?"

"You must agree to be our mate."

"Mate?" asked Cyn, flabbergasted. "Is that cat talk for wife?"

"Yeah," said Aris. "But not in a human sense. There is no divorce. If a mate dies, the surviving spouse can marry again, but other than that... it's practically forever."

"So, I'd be married to both of you? Forever?"

"Yes," said Kane.

"Will I be expected to do housework or cook? Because I don't do that kind of crap. Or knit. Or garden. Or grocery shop."

"It's not a subservient role," said Kane. "You would be our partner in all ways."

Cyn couldn't believe she was even considering this crazy

idea. She shook her head. "I guess being a werecougar is better than being a bloodsucker, but I was sorta resolved to the whole dying thing."

"Give us a chance. Maybe you'll find we're a better alternative to death." Kane motioned to Aris, who joined them on the bed.

Cyn's eyes widened. "You want me to sleep with you?"

"Not sleep," said Aris, his eyes turning cat-like. "Fuck."

10

K ane let out a long-suffering sigh. "Stay the night. Willingly. In the morning, if you decide not to mate with us, we'll let you go."

"What, exactly, does mating involve?"

"Biting," said Aris. He shucked his Nikes and socks, and then pulled off his shirt.

Cyn got a gander at his body, which she'd seen in the darkened forest, and in the glare of the hotel room lights it was even better. Her gaze flipped to Kane. He, too, was getting undressed. He was broader in the shoulders and chest than Aris, and probably a few inches taller. Both of them were handsome and muscled. And when she mentally put herself in the middle of that particularly tasty sandwich, her body went hot and tingly.

Hoo-boy.

"What about your heart?" asked Kane. "Will it fail if we... um, push it?"

"I exercise all the time and it's held so far. And if it fails during--" Aw, crap. Had she just admitted she was gonna do the naughty thing with them? "--er, during, you know, then hey, what a way to go."

"We go gentle," he told Aris. "After she becomes cougar, we'll play hard."

Cyn's stomach twisted. Play hard? Oooh. These were her kind of boys. But she hadn't necessarily decided to hitch herself to them for all eternity. So, they'd just have to play hard now, while she could enjoy it.

They took off their jeans and both climbed onto the bed.

Without another word of protest, she wiggled off her panties and unsnapped her bra. Then, naked, she crawled into the bed between them. Kane was the first to skim his palm down her side, splaying his long fingers over her abdomen. His hand was warm, and her skin contracted from the light contact.

Aris was obviously the impatient one. He kissed her. He was aggressive, plundering her mouth with his tongue and nipping at her lips. She cupped his face and gave back as good as she got, sucking on his lower lip before ravaging his throat. And when she found that vulnerable spot beneath his throat, she bit him.

The low growl sent chills straight through her. Excitement coiled. Oh, he was gonna hold back until Kane let him loose. She raked her nails down his back and licked the bruised skin. She turned more fully toward Aris, pressing against him, while Kane stroked the skin of her back, buttocks, thighs.

Aris's fingers tangled in her hair and he drew her up for another brutal kiss. She loved it. Heat streaked through her, leaving her flushed and yearning.

And when he put his teeth against her throat and growled, her womb contracted.

"God, you're wet," said Kane as he slipped his hand over her hips and delved into her swollen pussy. "She likes it."

Aris reached across her to touch Kane, and she turned, giving Aris her backside, and kissed Kane. Aris shifted so that his thick cock slid between her ass cheeks. She wrapped a leg around Kane, and he teased her weeping pussy with his sizable cock.

He bent to lave at her aching nipples, lightly biting the distended peaks. Pleasure shuddered through her.

Her senses whirled as the men worshipped her with hands and mouths. She could barely breathe. Barely think. She rolled again to face Aris and slid between his thighs so she could taste his cock.

He moaned, grabbing the bed covers in his fists, his eyes closing as she sucked his length into her mouth. She relaxed her throat, and took him all the way down to his balls.

"Damn," he managed. "Damn."

And as she sucked and licked on Aris's yummy cock, Kane positioned himself behind her, lifting her hips until she was kneeling with her ass up, and he -- thank the ever-loving gods -- pierced her swollen cunt. His penis filled her, stretching her to the limit.

"Oh, hell," she murmured.

It was an interesting rhythm. Kane plunging into her from behind, and Aris thrusting into her mouth. Nothing had ever felt so good. It was like she'd been searching for a place to belong her whole life, and she'd found it. Here, with them.

She felt Kane leaned down and sink his teeth into the back of her neck. Aris's teeth pierced the top of her breast. They bit her, growling, and she felt the energy around them snip and snap and then they bound. She knew it to the core of her soul.

"I'm going to come," cried Aris. "Cyn, baby. Please."

She grabbed his shaft at the base and suckled his quivering head. Then he was groaning, shouting, and shooting hot seed down her throat. She swallowed and swallowed, and sucked on him until he was dry.

And still Kane pounded into her. He'd forgotten gentle, thank heavens. Aris scooted out from underneath her, and she planted her hands on the bed, and closed her eyes.

Sparkling pleasure coiled in her womb. She could hardly draw in a breath. Then Kane cried out, and pierced her deeply. Damn. She felt his spasms as his come filled her.

Sweat dripped from her neck and splashed the coverlet. As Kane withdrew from her she collapsed to the bed, and rolled over. Before she could even complain -- *hello, where's my orgasm* -- Aris slid on top of her. He was as hard as a fucking steel rod.

Her surprised gaze met his smug one.

"Werecougars are a lusty bunch," he said. "Doesn't take long to recover. Plus, seeing Kane plow you really turned me on."

"Yeah, me, too," she said, yanking on his shoulders. "Now shut up and fuck me."

He wasted no time slipping inside her and stroking her into a frenzied rhythm. He tugged a nipple into his mouth and sucked on it, and pleasure made her gasp. She dug her nails into his ass and met his thrusts, and then stars exploded, and she felt like the whole world was spinning.

And then it was.

She felt her heart stall as her body seized.

Aris's face went white and then Kane was there, too, and she couldn't tell them thank you because it was getting dark.

Then there was nothing.

PART III

11

"She's alive," said Thomas. "But her heartbeat is weak."

"Too weak for my changing bite," added Gareth. "I'm sorry." He shared a look with Thomas, slightly shaking his head. It was too late to save the young woman draped on the couch, barely breathing.

The vampire looked sympathetically at the two were-cougars who appeared on their doorstep with a dying human female. Her name was Cyn, and she was a lithe and pretty young thing. Her life force draining away seemed such a shame. Now, the four men surrounded her like pallbearers, waiting for the inevitable moment of death.

Thomas was unsure about these people—especially after the males admitted they'd come to assassinate them all. The only reason he allowed them succor was because Gareth vouched for their honor. The werecougar had expected his brother to come after him eventually, but he seemed less worried about their confession and more concerned about protecting their mate. As he should. Thomas' own worry about her and their child made him less than eager to stick around the area. Angela was upstairs packing. They would leave as soon as possible—and find a better hiding spot.

"She's gonna die unless you change her," said the one called Aris. The young man looked at Kane, the bigger of the two men. They both stared down at the woman who was to be their mate. She was breathing erratically, her skin gray, and her lips tinged blue.

Thomas understood their pain. If anything ever happened to Angela, he would tear apart the whole world to save her.

"I suggest y'all do something," said a honeyed voice from the doorway. Thomas looked up. Angela practically glowed with vitality. And she was nearly full term. Her small hands rested on her rounded tummy, causing Thomas' undead heart to turn over in his chest. "C'mon," she said to him and Gareth. "She needs help. Thomas?"

He could not deny Angela's request. She was his conscience—his very soul. "I can attempt to change her," said Thomas. "But I don't know if she'll survive it."

"She's already dying," said Angela. "You must try, sugar."

Thomas nodded. "Very well then."

Kane lifted Cyn to a seated position. Thomas sat on the edge of the couch and brought her close, so that his mouth rested on the point between her neck and shoulder blade.

He sprouted sharp fangs.

Then he leaned down and bit Cyn.

The air began to fill with gold sparks, and then this magic flowed between Thomas and Cyn, and when he finally let her go, her skin was bleeding and bruised. And she was still gray and limp.

The gold magic hung in the air as Thomas raked a nail across his wrist and pressed it again Cyn's mouth. "She only needs enough to bind her blood to mine."

Cyn weakly sucked on his wrist, but she didn't open her eyes. She soon fell back against Kane, shuddering deeply. Thomas rose from the couch and Aris instantly took his place, stroking the woman's short black hair. "What now?" Aris asked.

"Now," said Thomas. "We wait."

12

When Cyn woke up, she was pinned between two men on a really comfortable bed. Aris and Kane held her as though she was fragile, but she felt the opposite. She felt strong. Wonderful. Different.

"Where are we?" she asked.

"Heaven," said Aris. "Isn't it obvious?"

"I expected less cats."

Kane chuckled. "I'd say she's back." He stroked her cheek. "We're in a safe place. For now. We have much to talk about, sweetheart. But it can wait."

Cyn nodded. Her senses were crazy-sharp. She could smell them. Her boys. Not unpleasant scents. Kane was sandalwood, rich and sweet. And Aris... his scent was a little like hot peppers—spicy and pungent. She tried to draw in a deep breath, to take more of them in, and her lungs refused to expand. Wait a damned minute.

"My heart's not beating," she said. "What the hell?"

"Cyn." Aris's blue gaze caressed her face. "You're okay."

"Did you miss the part where my heart's not beating?"

He put a hand against her chest. Despite its lack of beats, she felt healthy. Holy shit. Kane put his hand over Aris's and Cyn felt some serious warm fuzzies.

"What happened?"

"You're vampire now," said Kane apologetically. "You weren't strong enough for Gareth's bite to become werecat. We had no choice."

Sure, they did. They could've let her die and been on their way. But these men, these shifters, had saved her. Could it be possible that she'd found her way to love?

"If you prefer," said Aris, "we could stake you."

"Smart ass." She smiled. "Hey, I'm breathing—well, I'm not breathing, but I'm still here on the planet. That's fine by me."

These two men wanted her. She had love blossoming right here, right now. From death to second chance ... damn, she was lucky.

Kane kissed her. When he was done turning her into Jell-O, Aris took his turn. As they made love to her, Cyn thought about the future, a real future with two men who would protect her fiercely and love her for always.

Beating or not, her heart belonged to Kane and Aris, along with her body, mind, and soul.

Not bad.

Not bad at all.

ALL BY MY SASS

#2 THE PRIDE COMMANDS

1

A bby Shafer stood in the long line of women and wished this scenting ceremony was over with. Seriously, the Valiant werecougar colony relied too heavily on traditions that were no longer relevant. Like when the new alpha and all the other bachelors chose mates from all the eligible females in their small colony. The rest of the world did things like dating and falling in love— but the shifter communities were all, "Let's sniff each other and see how that works out."

She tapped her foot on the wood floor thinking about how being viewed and chosen like a steak in a display case was less romance and more grocery store. Why not just go to the Gardner General Store and stand in the deli section with all the rest of the meat?

She looked around the room feeling more and more antsy. Her mother, who sat next to Daddy in the second row of the pews filled with proud parents, stared at her with brows furrowed. The look in her gaze was: *Stop fidgeting.* Her dad's expression echoed the same sentiment.

Crap. Abby inhaled a steadying breath and tried to keep her impatience from manifesting as jittery movement.

Abby couldn't help but think about her life. She had been the fifth child. The only girl. The weakest one born to her family. Some werecougars left weak kittens in the woods -- either to die or to prove they had the strength to survive. But even though she was a mewling, tiny thing, her family chose to keep her. She was nurtured by them. Loved, but not coddled. They expected her to pull her weight. To do as well as her bigger and stronger brothers. To take care of herself.

They also prepared Abby to take her expected place in the Valiant Colony. Her father was among the cougars that patrolled the borders of their territory. He was an enforcer —considered what humans called blue-collar workers, and not part of the upper echelon. Yet he seemed satisfied with his life. In fact, her whole family seemed happy with their lives. But as the youngest child of cougars with lesser rank, expectations for her future were mundane and common. Either she followed her mother into administrative work or she joined her father as an enforcer.

All of them were taught to fight at a young age. Abby learned to defend herself, but she wasn't one to seek violence when cleverness and intelligence could more easily win the day. Her curiosity made her unafraid to ask questions. To dream bigger. To want more. Her heart yearned for freedom, but her familial duty kept her compliant.

So, when Reese Valiant assumed leadership as the new alpha, custom dictated that all the singles had to mingle. Abby felt anxious, excited, worried, and scared.

Reese Valiant was a little broody and a lot sexy. Abby had watched him from a safe distance since she'd hit puberty and knew what it was to desire. But she had no pie in the sky dreams that Reese would pick her. No alpha in his right mind would want Abby. She was what her Mom called "voluptuous," which really meant she was thick and curvy. Aside from not being a skinny ninny, her family was too low in rank. So, she wasn't a serious contender.

Not being considered competition had its advantages. While she was growing up, other girls rarely picked on her. Of course, that may have been because she had four protective older brothers who were handsome and more than willing to satisfy the bedroom urges of willing females. And they did not take kindly to slurs against their little sister. The long-held rule of "I can pick on my sibling, but you can't," was very much gospel in their family. Abby had gotten used to being ignored, even looked at with pity. She didn't care about the opinions of others, anyway. She didn't need their approval.

She was only here to please her parents—at least that's what she told herself. They knew how she felt about the colony's archaic expectations. But still... she hadn't wanted to disappoint them. They'd always loved and cared for her, even when traditions dictated otherwise, and she figured it would cost her nothing to honor this one small aspect of colony life. However, she refused to acknowledge the niggling worm of hope that she might catch a certain man's scent over the course of the night.

Reese was too intuitive for a male, especially for an alpha male. In the old days, his choice to think rather than to act would've made him appear weak. But anyone who knew him knew Reese Valiant was every ounce an alpha. He'd proven himself time and time again in physical and mental agility. He broke long-held records for both physical acumen and strategy. His father had been alpha, and Reese had been the firstborn. Even so, no one could say he hadn't earned his place.

The door opened, startling Abby, and in strode Reese Valiant. Her heart fluttered at the sight of him. A few inches over six feet tall, golden amber eyes, dark hair cut short, and a jaw so sharply square it could probably saw a board in half —yeah, the man was drool-worthy. Add to that all those muscles tucked into a custom-tailored suit and fancy shoes, and you had all the sexy you could want.

Except she didn't. Okay, okay, she did, but he was way out of her league. Reese had gone to an Ivy League school so he had brains in that yummy package, too. Well, what did it matter? Every other female in the line seemed ready to swoon, and many of them were more his match. They were dressed to the nines: wearing high heels to lengthen the calves, short dresses to hint at their firm thighs, material cinching their trim waists, cleavage to showcase pert boobs, make-up to highlight sharp cheeks and full lips, and enough hairspray to peel away the earth's ozone layer.

When she dressed this morning, she stopped short of shoving herself into one of her brothers' hockey shirts, a pair of jeans, and her favorite Converse sneakers. But, you know, the parent thing again. So, she'd brushed her hair until it shone and wore it long and straight. She'd been blessed with creamy, blemish-free skin—yay, Shafer genetics—so she only put on eyeliner and mascara and lip gloss with a hint of sparkle. She wore a simple green dress that swirled around her knees and a pair of nude flats. She didn't own high heels.

"And you are?"

Abby looked up into the golden gaze of Reese Valiant. Shit. He'd already gone through half the line? Her heart nearly leapt out of her chest. *Why are you talking to me*? Maybe he'd mistaken her for a server. *Say hi to the man and let him move on, you dolt.*

"Abby Shafer." Unnerved by his stare, she thrust out her hand. "Nice to meet you."

The women on either side of her gasped, and she realized she'd just made a huge mistake. *You have to at least act submissive to the alpha,* said her mother. *Keep your eyes down, try to smile, and say nothing unless he talks to you.*

Reese took her hand and grasped it. His fingers were strong and warm and that otherwise polite touch sent an electric shiver straight through her.

"Reese Valiant." He let go of her hand and smiled. "But you probably knew that."

"Didn't have a clue," she answered. "I thought I was in line to meet the alpha." She leaned forward. What the hell, right? She was already in trouble. "I hear he's going to pick a bride the same way I pick ripe fruit."

His smile turned into a laugh. He took her hand once more and pulled her forward. To her shock—not to mention the shock of everyone else—he proclaimed, "I have chosen."

Not: I have chosen her. And her. And her. And her, too.

Not: I have chosen. Ha, ha! Just kidding!

He'd said, with complete confidence, "I have chosen."

No contest. No other choices. No challenges to be met.

Just... I have chosen.

"Are you insane?" Abby whispered, staring up at him. "I'm the least qualified woman here to mate with you." She frowned, leaning closer still and keeping her voice low. "I don't wear high heels. Or make-up. And I'm terrible about being submissive. I don't know the first thing about being an alpha's mate. I am trouble. Just ask my mother. Are you sure you don't want to look again?"

"Why would I look at the other fruit?" he teased. "I've already found the perfect plum."

The bright moon pierced the darkness the beautiful mess of trees, moss, and marsh, the forest in Southeast Texas was the sovereign domain of the werecougars running and leaping through the muggy July night.

Two by two, the werecougars split off, yowls echoing through the dense woods as shifters engaged in mating.

Two of those cougars, one larger than the rest with golden fur and a smaller one with darker fur, more on the side of dirty sunshine.

They reached a small clearing. To the left was the entrance to a cave. Abby followed Reese into the dark space. The male cat loped ahead and Abby paused, shifting into her human form. Her heart trilled. Holy crap. Mating with the alpha. This had to be a dream, because reality had always been a bleak bitch.

"Abby."

She followed Reese's voice, its gentle demand guiding her. The alpha lounged by the fire, reclining on thick blankets, waiting for her.

"Is this part where you tell me this is all just a prank?"

"Yes," he said drily. "I picked you as my mate and led you to this romantic and private spot so that I could yell *gotcha*."

"Well, that makes more sense than mating with me." There had to be some alternate explanation for why Reese had chosen her. "Are you off your meds?"

He smiled. "Are you always so...difficult?" He ran a finger along his chest, and Abby's pussy warmed with slick heat.

"Yes." She swallowed at the dry knot in her throat. "Trouble, remember?"

"Come here," he said, his voice low and husky. "Let me show you how much I want you, Abby Shafer. Trust me."

Deliciously naked, his long, thick cock nestled in the dark curls between his legs; Abby felt her knees and her resolve weaken. She wanted to trust him, more than anything.

She took a tentative step forward. "This is happening. Really freaking happening," she murmured.

"Yes, it is," agreed Reese. He held out his hand. "Come. Join me."

Abby nodded. She crawled onto the furs into the arms of her strong, handsome alpha.

He smiled. "I'm going to kiss you, Abby. And after that, I'm going to taste you. Mark you. Make you mine."

She gulped—terrified to answer. Terrified she'd ruin the moment. His hot lips pressed against her mouth, and she parted for him, inviting the invasion of his tongue. Tingles of excitement raised gooseflesh on her skin as his hands cupped her breasts, his thumbs sliding against her rigid nipples.

She groaned.

Reese pulled back to gaze into her eyes. "I love how your body reacts to my touch. I can smell the musk of her desire, your need." He slid a finger between the folds of her sex. "You're so wet and warm."

He took his lust-slickened finger and rubbed her juices over her nipples, and then one by one, he licked the taut nubs. His raspy tongue swirled and teased her.

"Please," she begged, her fingers winding through his thick hair. "Yes. More."

He smelled like earth, like smoke, like rain.

"Tell me what you want?"

"You know," she begged.

"I want to hear you say it. I want to hear that I'm your choice as well. Do you choose me?"

"Yes, Reese. I choose you." In that moment, she would have said anything to have him take her, to have him inside her. Even so, she knew the truth of her words as she said them. "I want you in me. I want this. You."

"Then you will have me." His smooth flesh slid along hers as he wrapped his arms around her and kissed her breathless. His tongue danced with hers, mimicking the movement of his cock as he parted her legs and slid his hard length into the soft wetness of her sex.

She wound her legs around his waist, stretched by his thick shaft, the pain like background noise against the pleasure, and matched his thrusts, her hands clutching his hair, her mouth attacking his with fervor.

"Oh yes," she cried. "Yes!"

She hadn't known what to expect. She'd had boyfriends, but sex had never been super exciting. All right, *two* boyfriends. And neither one made her feel this way, the way she felt with Reese, not even once. And Reese was going to mark her.

He slid his arms under her back then he rolled over. She sat on top of him; his cock embedded inside her, and inhaled a steadying breath. She was so greedy for him. She trembled with need.

The emotions lighting his gaze reflected what was in her heart.

With eager anticipation, she planted her hands on his chest and moved, stroking his cock with her inner muscles.

"My sweet Abigail. My beautiful mate." He grabbed her hips and shoved his cock deeply inside her, pushing her closer to the brink of ecstasy. "More, my love, give me more."

Flesh slapped against flesh.

Moans echoed in the cave.

The shadows of flames danced on their sweaty, nude bodies.

Pleasure spiked in her belly, filling her core with the first tendrils of bliss. He filled his hands with her breasts, kneading the flesh. She pushed her clit against him, rubbing harder and faster, slamming herself onto his cock. His nimble fingers flicked her sensitive nipples then lightly twisted the nubs.

The orgasm bloomed into sparks of heat and joy that took her hostage, and hinted at the pleasure that waited. She panted, fucking him with frantic movements, wanting the same glorious end for them both. His hoarse cry of completion sent her flying over the edge. They came together, with a splendid violence, and Reese pulled her down and sank his teeth into her neck.

She was bitten.

And she now belonged only to the alpha.

2

One year later...

O   *ne year later...*
      Abby Valiant looked out the picture window, nerves frayed and body exhausted. The dim yellow of the porch light barely penetrated the darkness, but with her werecougar vision she saw the still falling flakes continue to build the hip-deep snow.

The cabin was isolated, one of several rentals near the lake. She couldn't remember the name of the town or the highway—or hell, even which state she'd been driving across. Earlier in the day, she'd white-knuckled driving in the blizzard, but still managed to see the sign for the cabin rentals. The woman manning the single desk in the tiny office was chatty, friendly. She said only one other cabin had been reserved. She happily relayed that Abby's closest neighbors were an elderly couple celebrating their fiftieth anniversary by staying in the same cabin where they'd honeymooned.

Fifty years. What she wouldn't give to have five whole decades with Reese. Had they been a normal couple, she could've looked forward to another hundred years with him. Shifters were long-lived.

Usually.

Her gaze drifted through the tall pines and to the iced-over lake. It looked like a ghost floating in the velvet night. Nothing stirred. Nothing natural, but she knew the Hunter would be out there. The memory of the day Reese chose her to be his mate surfaced. He'd enjoyed riling her ever since— to bring out that feisty spirit, he would say. But that moment, when she'd questioned his sanity he said: *That was the moment I fell in love with you. My heart was yours.*

And she believed him. Because after that look, that smile, that night in the cave—her heart was his, too.

Regret clawed at Abby. She stifled a sob and swept her gaze over the cabin. The place was basically one large room. The front door opened into the living area, which consisted of an overstuffed brown couch and one end table. A single brass lamp with its tan shade looked ready for a garage sale. The couch faced a large, stone fireplace. A cheery fire burned inside the hearth. She didn't want the fire's cheer or its warmth, but survival instincts could be strong—even for a woman who had every intention of sacrificing herself.

Abby walked into the kitchenette with its small stove, narrow refrigerator, and tiny metal sink. There was a little table and two chairs parked to the right.

The fridge held bottled water and a few condiments. The rental fees had included stocked dry goods as well as dishes, glasses, silverware, and cookware. A thick patchwork quilt covered the king-sized bed. The four blue-checkered pillows were propped against the headboard. It looked welcoming, but she didn't want the bed's comfort. She wanted Reese, but that wasn't possible. Not anymore.

The door to the left of the bed led to the bathroom. Like

everything else in the cabin, it was small. Almost too small for the sink, toilet, and shower crammed into the space.

Her gaze lingered on the bed. Abby couldn't curl up in that cozy space... not without thinking about the last time she'd seen Reese.

Reese. Now that she'd had time to process what had happened, what she'd done in reaction to her infertility, she was scared. Not that she thought she'd made the wrong choice—she'd done the only thing she could do. If she hadn't traded places, the Hunter would've come for her husband.

In the Valiant colony, there was one belief held by all: The colony was protected by one of its first ancestors. The Hunter. Every year while most of the world celebrated All Hallow's Eve, the werecougars of Valiant called upon the Hunter. To show homage. To give thanks. To renew shifter strength.

And that's when the Shaman pulled her aside and told her the bad news: the Hunter was displeased with the alpha's inability to have an heir. That hadn't been Reese's fault.

It was hers.

Abby rubbed her arms, chilled despite the heat emanating from the crackling fire. The waiting was killing her. After the Shaman had performed the spell needed to trade Abby's life for Reese's, she'd left Texas quickly. She hadn't wanted her death to be in the colony's territory. At least that's what she told herself. Some small, cowardly part wanted Reese to find her. To save her.

Which was pointless. Because he was determined to keep her as his mate. The water splashed Abby's hand, and she looked down. When had she started to fill the teakettle? She shut off the water then put the kettle onto the burner and turned it on. Next, she opened the cabinet looking for a snack she didn't really want. But such mundane tasks couldn't take her mind off Reese.

The night of the argument, in their bedroom, the ghosts of their grief hadn't tempered their lovemaking. Certainly they'd both been haunted by all the visits to various doctors, obstetricians, and fertility specialists, but it hadn't stopped Reese from taking control.

She closed her eyes and remembered their last time together. The last time she lay with him in their marriage bed.

~

T*hree weeks earlier...*

"No, Abby. I will not divorce you," Reese said as he stood in their kitchen. "I will not choose another mate."

"You're stubborn!" she cried.

He calmly prepared tea, ignoring her vibrating anger. The way he moved, graceful and deliberate, simply ratcheted up the anguish clawing her throat.

"Every alpha has been born from your family. Your bloodline... it's sacred. Important."

"It's not more important than you."

"Yes, it is."

He stopped pouring the water and turned toward her. In that moment, she'd seen the truth flash in his eyes. His own heartbreak. The knowledge that the wife he loved could not bear him the heir he needed.

Her grief washed over her again. She had failed him. Her body had failed him. She couldn't have his children. He had chosen the wrong female, because the stupid fool listened to his heart.

He strode forward and gathered her into his arms. He held her tightly until she relented and accepted his comfort. She wrapped her arms around his waist and wept. His grasp tightened, and his chest heaved as he leaned down to press his face against her hair. Together, they grieved for the family they would never have.

Abby taken by the moment, and still fully clothed, sank to her knees. Reese, needing to control and uncontrollable situation, warned her to not make eye contact unless he gave her permission. He removed a pillowcase and rolled it lengthwise and used it to bind her hands behind her back.

He undressed, removing each piece of clothing casually, as if he had all the time in the world. He ignored her, neither looking at her nor coming near her. His blatant dismissal had been designed to thin her patience while it increased the desperate wanting that pulsed through her.

By the time Reese stood naked before Abby, she hungered for the slightest look of approval or the merest whisper of recognition. Aching need curled through her, conquering her despair.

Reese stepped so close his toes brushed the tips of her knees. Then he demanded, "Suck me. I want to feel your mouth on my cock."

Giving a blowjob on her knees without the help of her hands was awkward at first. But she got him hard and made him tremble under the onslaught of her tongue, teeth, and lips.

He pulled away from her, his thighs shaking. However, his expression was placid. He moved behind her and grasped the pillowcase binding her. He led her to their massive dresser and untied her. "Bend over and put your palms flat against the top."

Without question, she pressed her hands against the solid, beautifully carved wood. He pulled down her jeans and her silk panties. His fingers, slightly trembling as he controlled his lusts, grazed her hips.

He rested the tip of his length at her slick opening for no more than a breath before he slid his thick shaft into her wet heat. She thought the rocketing sensation might kill her.

He fucked her without mercy, telling her unequivocally that she was not allowed to come. Being told not to find pleasure had the opposite effect. Bliss coiled tight and hard, threatening to send her over the edge with every rough stroke of his cock.

Reese came, his fingertips biting into her hips as his cries of completion filled her ears. For a long moment, there was nothing but the harsh sounds of his panting and her own low, needy whimpers she couldn't silence.

"Stand up."

She did as he demanded. She was overwhelmed by the need he inspired. She loved him so much. So. Much. Her body was damp with sweat and quivering with desire. His hands coasted over her belly, down her thighs, and around her ass.

But he denied his touch where she wanted it the most. Her swollen, drenched pussy.

"You are so beautiful, so responsive," he whispered. "You are my wife, Abby. I will not lose you."

His thumb brushed her clit and pleasure jackknifed. Two fingers danced along her tender folds then dipped inside her. She felt the erotic press of those digits on her G-spot.

Reese pushed her to the brink. He was ruthless. His

thumb stroked her tortured sex while he worked two fingers inside her. She bit her lower lip, begging her own body not to give in. Not until he told her.

"Come for me, Abby."

Her orgasm was instantaneous, the pleasure so intense she lost her ability to breathe, to think. Her legs collapsed. Only his arm wound around her waist kept her upright as her body convulsed. His lips pressed against her neck and his hard body cradled hers as she rode the wave to fulfillment.

$\approx$

T he whistle of the kettle startled Abby out of the delicious and painful memory. She got out a mug and a tea bag then turned off the burner and poured the hot water.

Shifters were not like humans. They didn't just worry about themselves as individuals. She and Reese were not an ordinary couple who, faced with infertility, might choose to adopt. Other shifters had different methods for breeding, but in the Valiant colony, bloodlines were important. For genetics, yes, but also to continue an alpha's line, which was sacrosanct. For all her thumbing her nose at traditions and the archaic beliefs of her community, especially in the modern world, she wanted the honor, the duty of carrying the alpha's child. But beyond that, she wanted to have Reese's baby.

And she could not. And that flaw had endangered the man she loved. There was no turning back now. Prayers were for the dying. The living were expected to handle their own problems.

The shame of not being able to produce children would

undermine Reese as the alpha. Her barrenness would dishonor her family, too. At the very least, they would be ridiculed, and at the worst, they would endure abuse, maybe even expulsion. Not even Reese would be able to shield her family. No one would listen to him if they found out he'd put his love for her over the needs of the colony. Her mate would lose everything, because he was too stubborn to do the right thing.

The ache in her chest weighed so heavy on her that she slumped onto the couch. She had no destination when she left. She'd just drove—randomly taking roads without purpose or direction. She only stopped for gas when the tank was empty, for sleep when exhaustion overwhelmed her, and to eat when her stomach became so gnarled with hunger she felt lightheaded and nauseous. She had wandered a confusing path so that finding her would be difficult if not impossible for Reese. But the Hunter would find her. Of that, Abby had no doubt.

And tonight, she'd finally stopped running.

The Hunter would come soon, and she almost preferred facing the ancestral spirit rather than her furious, worried spouse.

Almost.

3

R eese Valiant drove through the blinding snow. His fingers gripped the steering wheel so hard, his knuckles turned white. After Abby left, the day after their All Hallow's Eve celebration, it didn't take long to wrangle a confession from the Shaman. To protect the colony, the Hunter would kill him and chose another alpha—one that might well not be a Valiant. He'd nearly torn the man's head off his neck when he revealed he'd bonded Abby to the Hunter. She would give her life so that he could live and mate again.

He wanted to do things different than the alphas before him, but he knew bringing the colony fully into modern times would be a slow process. That's why he'd chosen the town's only judicial building, the courthouse, for the day of the scenting, and insisted the women remained dressed. The proceeding took place in the largest courtroom, the judge on standby to perform the human tradition of marriage for him and his mate.

Reese had noticed Abby first among all the eligible females in the room. She was curvy with a bright, curious gaze and an energy that drew him like a moth to the flame. She was so beautiful he couldn't take his eyes off her. She had dressed well, but not provocatively. Her simple dress showed off her sweet curves. She'd worn black shoes, flat and comfortable, rather than trying to totter on high heels. She hadn't tried to be sexy, offering bedroom eyes or knowing smirks, or posturing with wiggling hips and thrust-out breasts. Her long, silky hair was worn straight, shoulder-length, in a very no-nonsense way. She had straight-cut bangs that touched her eyebrows, and she'd worn very little makeup. Later, when he introduced himself, he could smell the light floral scent of her perfume and the faint hint of strawberries of her lip balm.

It was her lack of artifice that had made him notice her. Truth be told, though, he'd noticed her long before then. She kept her head down and did her work, but her occasional looks his way hadn't gone unnoticed, and no matter what clothes she wore, her sexy curves hadn't escaped his attention as well. He'd wondered many times what she would look like naked, and he hadn't been disappointed.

The night of the scenting ceremony, Abby had looked around the room in open curiosity, her gaze cataloging the architecture and the furniture. She hadn't glance at the other women, who sized each other up while they tried to make goo-goo eyes at him.

Reese had worked his way down the line, not really listening to introductions, and ignored the bold touches on his arms and hips as the other females vied for his approval.

When he'd finally reached her, she'd looked him in the eye, and held out her hand. She'd given a firm handshake, answered his questions point-blank, and teased him without a thought about his rank. He'd heard the pounding of her heart. It had matched his own.

Reese's phone beeped, turning his thoughts to the present. As part of the colony's revamping of security, tracking devices had been placed on the alpha's cars. Abby didn't know about the trackers, or she would've never taken the SUV. Despite knowing where she was, he'd been unable to catch up to her. She'd been running non-stop, and he couldn't predict her moves. The red dot on his phone verified that she was only ten miles away. She hadn't moved for about an hour, and he hoped it wasn't because she ditched the car or worse, the Hunter had caught up with her. He was so close now. His pulse raced with a mixture of anxiety and anticipation.

Abby was the missing part of his soul.

His other half.

His mate.

And nothing, no rules or traditions, or summoned spirit, would keep them apart.

Abby stretched on the couch, tucked a worn pillow under her head, and drew the quilt over her body. She stared at the flickering flames, watching them dance as the wood crackled. She drowsed there, her eyelids eventually drifting closed.

She slept deeply, dreaming of her husband, of the baby they would never have, when the child started wailing.

The wailing turned into screaming—inhuman sounds she'd never heard before.

Abby jolted awake.

The lamp on the nightstand glowed brightly, but the fire had burned down to embers. Reluctantly slipping out from the warm quilt, she padded to the picture window next to the front door—the only window in the whole cabin. She flipped on the porch light and stared out in the darkness.

All she could make out from the gray mass of falling ice and snow was the spindly shapes of trees. Everything else, including the lake, was lost in the dark and the storm.

Was the Hunter out there?

Would it come for her now?

Her heart jumped into her throat, and she backed away from the window. Coward. She was such a fucking coward. She hadn't realized how much it would hurt to be without Reese.

Cords of wood were stacked next to the fireplace along with a pile of newspapers. A box of extra-long matches rested on the mantle. With all the tools at her disposal, Abby had a new fire going in no time.

She wished the window had curtains or blinds for privacy. Most people probably liked the view, but she wanted to feel covered. Protected. Watching the snowstorm encapsulate the cabin was like watching gravediggers bury her coffin.

A loud, fearsome roar echoed.

Abby froze.

Her werecougar instincts kicked in, and she whirled toward the front door, throwing it open to sniff at the wind.

The rusty scent of blood, and the sickening stench of death overwhelmed her.

The Hunter.

Even prepared, she couldn't hold back a gasp as a tall, gaunt creature emerged from the tree line. Its gray skin hung in tatters off blackened bones. Its eyes were desiccated hollows, and its mouth a ragged gap filled with sharp, gray teeth. The old rusted scent of blood clung to its awful form. Okay. That was not the same spirit that had shown up to the All Hallow's Eve party. But maybe this was its true form.

Abby fought to catch her breath.

This was it. The only way to make sure Reese stayed safe.

The Hunter rose to its full height, lifted its head, and emitted a blood-curdling scream.

Abby hurried to the bed where she'd shed her winter clothes earlier. She threw on a sweater, thick socks, and boots, but the heavy thud in her belly told her it was too late. Next, she shoved on her coat and pulled up its hood. Finally, she pushed her trembling hands into fitted gloves.

Where was the spirit? Why hadn't it come for her already? Why was it waiting? Why wasn't it busting down the door or crashing through the window?

Abby hurried back to the door and opened it again.

The Hunter was gone.

The biting wind and freezing snow battered her. She shut the door behind her and hurried off the porch. She sank to her knees. Damn.

As she slogged her way toward the tree line, she tried to prepare herself. She hoped it didn't hurt. And that it didn't take long. And that Reese would forgive her.

She entered the thickest part of the forest and trudged onward. "Hey!" she yelled "I'm here!"

Her jeans got soaked and snow wiggled into her boots and made her socks cold and squishy. Her heart raced and sweat dotted her brow. Vaguely she recalled that sweating in freezing weather was a bad sign. She'd overexerted herself, and in her human form she could get hypothermia if she didn't get into a warm environment and out of her wet things.

She reached the top of the slope and looked down at the

cabin. She rested against the nearest tree and tried to even out her breathing.

Neither her human nor cougar enjoyed the cold. She'd been a fool to venture out into the snowstorm. She turned around and headed down the slope toward her cabin. She couldn't see anything in the cursed whiteout, and it seemed her coat snagged on every tree or bush she passed. The wind howled so fiercely it chilled her to the bones.

The wind... or the Hunter?

As she stumbled out of the tree line, she whirled around and saw the gaunt gray figure stalking her through the trees.

You give your life for that of your alpha?

The voice, both male and female, was calm. Colder than the snow, it echoed inside her mind.

"I do," she said.

You honor the Valiant colony with your sacrifice and ensure its future. For this, your death will be merciful.

"Thank you." Abby's tears fell. She watched the creature stalk closer, slow and methodical, its eyeless gaze on her. *I love you, Reese. I love you.*

She felt hands on her shoulders, and then she was yanked backwards into the solid chest of a man who wrapped his muscled arms around her waist. He scooped her up and ran with her into the cabin, his long legs and strong body unimpeded by the snow.

Once inside, he put her down, slamming the door and locking it behind them.

The white ski mask covering his face muffled his voice, and his eyes were hidden behind goggles. But she'd known who it was the moment he'd put his arms around her. She'd recognized the scent of earth and wind. The scent of home and husband.

Reese.

"Hiding in here won't do any good," she said in a shaking voice.

"It's all we got, sweetheart." He went to the end of the couch and pushed it against the door as a barricade. He grabbed the other end of the sofa, and together, they pushed it against the door. "That window's a big problem. Maybe we could rip off the closet and bathroom doors and nail them across."

She looked out the window. "Where did the Hunter go?"

The monstrous spirit had disappeared before. Was it even real?

Make the alpha leave.

The Hunter's male-female voice echoed into her head, its demand fierce. Oh, it was real, all right. And it was apparently irritated that Reese had shown up and run off with its sacrifice.

Have you met my husband? she thought back at the creature. *I can't make him do anything.*

You will find a way. I'll return soon.

I'll be here. I won't go back on my word.

She felt the Hunter's approval, and it was a strange sensation, as though it had rewarded her with a gold star for choosing death. Now, it was courage she needed. That's what the Hunter expected. For her to act like an alpha's mate.

"Abby?" Her husband gripped her shoulders and lightly shook her.

She blinked and stared up at him. "The Hunter is gone. It doesn't want to harm you. So it left." She moved away from his embrace and felt his eyes on her as she took off the gloves and rubbed her ice-cold hands together. God, she was freezing. Her whole body shivered, and her teeth chattered. As she shucked off her coat and boots, she studied

Reese. His entire body was encased in white and gray camouflage—even his snow boots were white. She briefly wondered at the duffel bag slung over his shoulder.

"You talk to it?" He pushed back the hood and removed the goggles. The white ski mask came off, revealing the short black hair, chiseled good looks, and gleaming amber eyes of her husband.

"It projects its voice into my head."

"If the Hunter stays away because I'm here, then you'll be safe as long as I'm with you."

Stubborn man. The Hunter would lose patience with her husband. She'd felt the Hunter's reluctance to kill her mate, but it might decide that Reese was no longer good for the werecougars. Especially with his single-minded devotion to her.

He stared at her. "Why did you do it?"

"You know why." Abby sat on the couch and tugged off her socks. She couldn't stop shivering. Not all of it had to do with being cold. How could she get Reese to leave? How could she make him stop looking as though he couldn't decide whether to hug her or strangle her?

He took off his coat and draped it over the couch with a casualness that belied the fury in his eyes. Well, what had she expected? He wasn't going to thank her for leaving him, even if it was to save him and to make sure his line survived intact. He glared at her, arms crossed. He was probably counting all the reasons why he shouldn't kill her himself. But she knew his anger was rooted in his fear, his love.

"I must honor my pact with the Hunter. I'd prefer it if you weren't here."

"Too bad. I won't live without you, Abby." He strode to her and yanked her up by the arms. "You're everything to me," he said through gritted teeth. "You are more valuable than my blood line. More than my own life."

"You are worth a hundred of me!" she shouted. "You are the alpha. The colony needs you. It's duty. Don't you understand? You have a duty to our people that transcends anything you might feel about me. It is because I love you and the colony that I made this bargain. You will be stronger without me. Just let me go."

"I can't. I can't let you go. I need you." He let go of her arms and stepped back. She saw his vulnerability then. "You are my strength, Abby. My heart. If I cannot have you, I will have no one. There is only one mate for me. You. Even if you go through with this, if the Hunter takes you, I will follow you into the afterlife."

"You can't. If you don't take another mate, then my sacrifice is for nothing."

"That's what I'm telling you. You don't get to make bargains on my behalf. If any sacrifice is made for our people, it will come from me. Not you."

"I am your sacrifice."

His expression pinched as if she'd punched him in the gut. "You are too stubborn, too fierce, Abby. Your soul is like fire. And I need that. I need you." His voice broke. He sucked in a breath. "I'm a better alpha with you. We are the strongest together. You bring balance to the colony—and to me. I would have found a way. You should have trusted me."

That's what he'd been telling her, showing her, and she'd been in too much pain, too afraid to understand the words, the actions. She and Reese were two halves of a whole. He needed her as much as she needed him. Beyond everything—carrying on Reese's line—not wanting to be without him had driven her to desperation. To madness.

She hadn't considered that he wouldn't want to live without her, either.

"You're shaking so hard I can hear your teeth chattering."

Abby blinked up at Reese. Her cold, snow-soaked clothes had chilled her to the bone.

He offered his hand, and she took it. He pulled her to her feet. "C'mon, let's get you undressed."

"Yeah, I've heard that one before."

"Every time I get near you, I want you naked," he said, but his tone was so grumpy he seemed more resentful than enamored. But hell, did she blame him? "I'll run you a hot bath." He waited until she looked at him again. He held her gaze, and she saw his pain, his fear, his anger. "Then we'll talk."

4

Reese stood and watched at the window holding the AK-47 he'd retrieved from his duffel bag. The winter storm had fizzled, though lazy snowflakes still drifted from the black sky. He'd turned off the porch light. The Hunter would return--the only question was when.

He almost wished the ugly bastard would appear so he'd have something to do other than think about Abby. About her stupid, idiotic, moronic self-sacrificing ass ... he made a fist, the urge to punch something so strong. He understood why she'd done it. He did. But she hadn't understood that he could not live without her. It would be like living without breath, without heartbeat. He would've found a way to keep their colony going, even if it meant giving up the old ways.

Had she really believed that her life was so much less than his? Or that he would simply work through his grief until he could find a replacement wife with a working womb?

He uncurled his fist and sucked in a ragged, harsh breath.

In the kitchenette, Abby washed their dishes.

Earlier, they'd sat at the tiny table to dine on soup and grilled cheese. Underneath the oversized shirt--one of his, he noted--he'd watched the seductive sway of her breasts. The rigid points of her nipples revealed she was either cold or thinking about him. Maybe she was just thinking about what he was capable of doing to her. Neither of them tried to fill up the silence.

He wanted her. Even now, as he looked out into the snow-filled darkness and tried to keep his mind on business, his ears were tuned to her movements. He heard the patter of her socked feet on the hardwood floor. She stopped just behind him.

He turned to face her and nearly lost his ability to breathe. She looked vulnerable. He knew better, of course. She was strong. So strong. He drank in her face, the upturned nose, the elfin chin, and the sloped angles of her cheeks. Her hair wasn't a single color. Interspersed in the cocoa strands were glints of auburn and gold. Her gold eyes were flecked with green. They were too dark to be called hazel, but all the same her eye color was more complex than brown.

Plain adjectives didn't do her justice.

Her gaze strayed to the window. "It won't be back tonight." She bit down on her lower lip. Tonight. He could tell it was more information than she wanted to give him. But she had never been good with duplicity. She'd never hidden anything from him.

Except this.

His heart turned over in his chest.

"We have better ways to spend the time," he said.

She looked at him then. Desire heated her gaze. She dropped to her knees, her gaze on the floor.

He stared at the crown of her head and tried to restart his lungs. He needed to get it together, but the knot in his throat stalled his ability to speak. Her submission was always so sweet.

Reese dragged her to her feet. He claimed her with his lips, rejoicing when she melted into his embrace, accepting the rough assault of his kiss. His heart jackknifed and started a wild beat. Reese dragged down her jeans and panties, and she kicked them away. He walked her backwards, then turned her around and pushed her against the small counter space between the sink and the stove.

He was her alpha, she his mate, and by God, tonight he would remind her of their sacred, unbreakable bond.

Abby gasped as he thrust a finger inside her slick heat. She knocked the sugar bowl, tea box, and spoon off -- all of which tumbled to the floor. Her palms flattened against the laminate. She struggled for breath and her whole body trembled in anticipation.

"You are mine, Abigail. No one takes what's mine," he growled.

"Yes," she panted, the scent of need and desire thick in her sweat.

Reese fumbled with his jeans. Then his cock was sliding between her thighs and deeply within her.

One of his hands anchored on her hip, holding her firmly while he took her. The other hand reached for her breast, twisting her nipple, delighting in her groan of pleasure.

He slid his hand over her stomach and claimed her feminine core. He stroked her clit roughly, and knew from her breathy moans that she was very close to her peak.

He thrust into her hard. She cried out. He thrust again.

And again. Every bit of his rage, his disappointment, and his love, he sunk it into Abby with abandon. He was losing her. Maybe she was already lost. No. He would save Abby. He would find away. He gripped her hips, plunging himself in and out of her, losing himself to the grip of her pussy on his cock.

"Abby," he said, his voice raspy. "Don't leave me." He buried his face at the base of her neck, kissing her as he steadied his rhythm. "I love you."

"Oh, god," she moaned. She reached around, her claws digging into his ass. "I love y—Ah!" She orgasmed, and her pulsations squeezed hard on his cock.

He groaned as heat and pressure pooled to his groin. His back stiffened, and he rocked into her body, holding her arch, and letting go his climax. His pleasure was fierce. "Oh, Abby. Abby!"

After their shudders stopped, he leaned forward, resting his head between her shoulder blades.

For a long moment, they stood in the kitchen, panting and sweating.

"You are beautiful," he finally said as he withdrew from her. "I want to worship you."

Her shoulders quivered under the onslaught of his words. His cock was already hardening again. He rubbed the ridge of his shaft against her ass, thinking of all the ways he wanted to use it on her. *This may be our last night*, he thought. Because if they couldn't stop the Hunter, then they would die together.

As she straightened, he took her chin into his hand. "I love you, Abby."

"I love you, too, Reese."

Her eyes were already glazed with desire. His balls tightened. God, she was so incredibly responsive. If the Hunter didn't kill him, his raging lust for her would do the trick.

Reese turned her in his arms. Abby's tongue wetted her lower lip. He leaned down and swiped his own tongue across her mouth. "Get ready for me, babe."

Naked, Abby lay on her stomach on the quilt and awaited Reese. Her hard nipples poked into the soft material. Her skin prickled in the cold air. But she would be warm soon enough.

"While I love your ass, I want you to roll over for me, so I can see your fantastic breasts."

She complied instantly.

Reese smiled. Feral and danger. "Good. Now, stretch your arms above your head."

Abby did as she was told, anticipation warming her belly.

Reese rounded the bed and squatted down. He put leather, fleece-lined cuffs on each of her wrists, tightening the leather wraps. He picked up the short chain that connected them. "If you think you need to, you can break the chain."

But she wouldn't. And they both knew it.

Reese smiled, and then showed her the black leather mask designed to cover only her eyes. He tucked the strap over her head. She closed her eyes as he fit the mask against her face. The fur lining was soft, but having her vision taken away made her feel wary. She was completely vulnerable to Reese and his every sexual whim. That both titillated and terrified her.

Damn it. She loved it when he went all dominant on her,

but she also knew that in order to reap all the rewards, she had to trust him. Implicitly. And until this night, she thought she had. But maybe she'd never really allowed herself to trust Reese. Not completely.

Because you aren't good enough for him, that infernal internal voice told her. So, how can you trust a man who exercises such poor judgment? Crap. This was her fault. All of it. Well, not the infertility, but the current mess she was in with the Hunter. If she truly believed Reese was a sound alpha, she would have trusted him to make the right decisions for them instead of taking matters into her own hands.

But had she been right? After all, he was here, chasing her down, instead of being back home leading their colony.

She heard him moving around. With the sensory deprivation, her werecougar senses were super sensitive to every wisp of sound, from his heavy breaths to the rustle of sheets as he joined her on the bed.

"I want you to think about all the wicked, naughty things I plan to do to your body."

Her whole body quaked at his words. She craved him. His touch. His approval. His love.

Why on earth would she ever give him up? Why hadn't she fought harder for them? For love? Guilt settled into her belly like acid.

His hands snaked around her thighs. His mouth pressed against her very core. Then his wicked tongue tortured her. Sucked away the evidence of her desire. Teased her clit. His clever tongue darted in and out of her, the strokes rough and fast. Bliss coiled tight and hot. Just as another orgasm threatened to overwhelm her, Reese pulled away.

Abby bit her lip to keep from protesting.

Reese inserted two fingers inside her, and then started

licking her clit again. The thrust of his fingers matched the thrusts of his tongue.

Just as she would've tipped over the edge again, Reese withdrew his fingers and stopped the lovely tongue-lashing. Sweat dripped between her breasts, and her whole body felt on fire. She wanted relief, but at the same time, the denial of her pleasure only stoked her higher.

Reese kissed each of her hips and licked her belly. His tongue dipped into her navel and sucked out the moisture pearled in the tiny concave.

Without sight, every sensation was exponentially increased. He was so good at torturing her.

She loved it.

"I'm going to take you," he said in a low voice. His breath rolled over her left hip as he scraped his teeth across her flesh. Her heart stuttered as he stood up. He left for a brief moment. When he returned, he wasted no time fitting his cock against her slick cunt. He grabbed her waist and lifted her.

As he slid inside her, the thick girth of him stretching her wide, she wrapped her legs around his waist and placed her shackled wrists behind his head. Her arms clenched his shoulders.

Oh, God. She sucked in a steadying breath. She tightened her grip around his waist and neck and used what leverage she had to meet his thrusts.

Her tender breasts rubbed against his lightly furred chest, her distended nipples getting electric thrills with every raw movement.

Reese filled her, stroking her higher and higher.

"I want you to come," he roared. "Come on my cock."

Abby's orgasm exploded as waves of pleasure and pure

joy racked her body. She cried out when a second burst of ecstasy followed close on the heels of the first.

Reese's groan intertwined with her low cries, and then he pressed deeply inside her, his hands digging into her as he came. Unbelievably, she went over the edge again, her whole body aflame as she rode a third upsurge into bliss.

5

Abby awoke in absolute darkness. For a panicked moment she thought she was blind but then realized the fire in the cabin had gone out.

It's always darkest before the dawn. Her mother said that. Wait long enough and the sun will come up. You'll find your way again.

It was close to sunrise. The silence was eerie, almost expectant. She couldn't help but think of the Hunter. Was it outside? Waiting?

Or did they have more time?

She sensed Reese next to her in the bed. The man didn't snore. Was he close to perfect or what?

A warm male hand slid over her breast. Abby smiled as Reese rolled on top of her and lavished attention on her breasts.

He sucked her nipple into the warm cave of his mouth, flicking the aching tip with his tongue. She wrapped her legs around his and pushed her slickening heat against his hard length. He tormented her other breast as one of his hands drifted down her side.

His movements were lazy, each touch and kiss designed to stoke the fires slowly. She writhed under him, pressed his body where she could since she was denied touching him with her hands.

She enjoyed Reese's gentle conquering of her body. By the time his cock slid inside her, she was more than ready for his final subjugation.

He slid his arms under her shoulders and increased his rhythm. She wrapped her legs around his waist and met every thrust.

Reese adjusted his angle and pounded into her harder and faster. She felt electrified. The sweet tendrils of orgasm coiled tightly.

"Abby," he whispered hotly in her ear. "My beautiful mate."

She arched against him, crying out, as she spun higher into the glossy bliss.

Moments later, he joined her.

Even as she reveled in the aftermath of their lovemaking, Abby sensed something was wrong. The darkness was not so much outside, but all around them. She suddenly felt as though she couldn't breathe.

"Reese!"

He understood what she couldn't voice. He rolled off her and onto the floor.

The Hunter appeared in a flash of cold white mist.

Terror seized her. She finally managed a deep breath, which she used to scream. She heard the Hunter screech. Its bony feet scrabbled on the floor as it ran toward the bed.

Where the hell was Reese?

"You have to go," she cried out. "Run, babe!"

"No!"

Panic had her twisting on the bed. She saw the tiny flare

of light before her ears registered the pistol's report. In that brief flash, she saw the tattered face of the Hunter.

"A gun won't stop it. Just... just let me go, you stubborn ass!"

"Never!" he yelled.

You're right, Abigail. He is stubborn.

Don't hurt him!

He made his choice.

The Hunter was nearly to the bed. Reese, naked and magnificent, fired directly into the creature's face until his gun was emptied. The Hunter screeched and moaned, scratching at its face. Abby heard the metallic ring of bullets falling off of its skull onto the floor.

"Reese!"

"Get off the bed, Abby. Run!"

Abby heard the sickening crunch of fists meeting flesh, snapping bone. Reese's thick cry of pain jolted her. Damn it! She rolled off the bed and onto the floor. She heard the vicious connection of fist against flesh. She flinched. Who'd gotten in that punch? The low groan was male. Reese!

Heart pounding and palms sweaty, Abby stood and snapped on the lamp.

The Hunter had Reese by the throat, and it was squeezing the life out of him. Reese struggled against the pressure crushing his neck, but she could see it was a losing battle. He tried to shift, but somehow the Hunter's torment kept her husband in a half-changed state.

Please, Hunter! Please, spare him! I will go with you. You can have me, my soul, whatever it is you want.

Its sightless gaze found hers. The Hunter's heavy sigh infiltrated her mind. *You are both stubborn. You fight well. You love more than any I have known before. Such qualities benefit the colony.*

I cannot have the alpha's babies. I am barren. That's why I offered my life for his.

I understand. It is too bad you do not have more faith in your mate.

I do! I do have faith in him. Please, please don't do this. Let him go.

Do you trust him, Abigail? Do you trust that he made the right decision in choosing you as his mate?

Did she? She loved him fiercely. And the way he'd tracked her down, and the way he'd restaked his claim and renewed their bonds the night before, she believed he'd loved her just as much. She was willing to sacrifice herself for him, and he was more than willing to do the same. Maybe an afterlife together was the right thing. Better than no life together. That kind of devotion, it couldn't be wrong.

It wasn't wrong, damn it. "Yes," she said aloud. "I trust that he made the right choice. I am the only woman he could have chosen. I am his mate, and if the Valiant line dies with us, than that is what is meant to be."

The Hunter tilted its head. Then it released Reese, who fell to the floor like a bag of bricks. Her husband flopped onto his side and clutched his throat. His wide gaze was on her, fear and love colliding in his amber eyes, but he was obviously incapacitated. He opened his mouth, but no words came out.

"I love you!" she cried.

The Hunter pinned her against the wall, then it put one large, bloody hand on her stomach. Its skeletal fingers pressed against her flesh. She felt searing heat all the way to her spine.

She closed her eyes. This was it. She would be sacrificed.

You will let him live?

Yes, said the Hunter.

The heat flared, and she gasped. She hadn't thought about how she would die. But death by this internal fire was ... was terrible. When would it be over?

She choked back a cry.

The Hunter stepped back and removed its hand from her belly. When she opened her eyes she saw a grandmotherly figure standing where the fearsome creature should be.

"Hunter?" she asked.

The old woman rolled her eyes. "You kill a few bad guys now and then and suddenly," she paused and waved her hands, "you're the Hunter. *Oooh*." She smiled. "I come in all forms, child."

"Yeah, well that last one was really awful."

"Look, when you're running down a sacrifice, you have to be scary. You think anyone would take me seriously as a grandma?"

"Good point." Abby swallowed. "That reminds me—am I dead?"

"Are you dead?" The woman laughed. "No, you darling idiot. The members of the colony, especially your moron Shaman, have forgotten that I am the protector spirit. Protection covers a lot of ground. And includes healing." She pointed at Abby's belly. "I have given you a gift. Now you can have the alpha's babies."

"What?"

"Sacrifice is not noble if it is not necessary." The Hunter smiled then she tapped the spot where Abby's heart beat like a primal drum. "Trust in love. Always."

The Hunter offered her a final, regal nod ... and then it faded into smoke and drifted away.

"Abby," whispered Reese. He'd gotten to his knees and he looked as though the color had been bleached from his skin.

"It's okay," she said. She kneeled beside him and stroked the hair away from his sweaty brow. She took Reese's hand and put it on her stomach. "The Hunter healed me."

Reese leaned in and kissed her fiercely. "Don't ever pull this shit again," he said.

"I won't," she promised. She glanced at the bed. "You want to make a baby now?"

"Yes," he said, grinning. "Hell, yes."

I'LL SASS IF I WANT TO

1

"Hellion Hill?" Cyn Salias' skepticism showed in her voice as the driver of the mini-van, vampire Thomas Moore, took the turn-off to their so-called safe place. Since the town was accessed by a questionable road that wound through dense woods, Cyn assumed the only people who ventured down this way were either lost or crazy. "Who names their town Hellion Hill?"

"Someone with a shitty sense of humor," commented Aris, her handsome werecat mate. He had blue eyes, wavy brown hair, and a wicked smile.

"Or someone who wishes to warn away others," said Kane, Cyn's other handsome werecat mate. Kane was taller and broader than Aris, his eyes dark and his frame almost too large to fit comfortably in the minivan. A girl with two powerful shifters bonded to her had very little to worry about. The fact she was a bad-assed assassin—if she did say so herself—made them a strong trio. And they'd partnered with another strong trio: vampire Thomas, werecat Gareth Harper, and their human mate Angela Ross. Between the six of them they'd stayed well ahead of the werecat asshole and the bitch vampire tracking them.

"Lord-a-mercy," said Angela in her honey-smooth Southern voice. She sat in the seat ahead of them, trying to get comfortable. She was nine months pregnant and could go into labor at any second, so Cyn doubted the woman could find any spot restful. "I'd kill for some ice cream. I could eat a whole gallon of chunky caramel chocolate."

"What about pickles?" teased Cyn.

"Yuck. I didn't like pickles when I wasn't preggers. No way is a child of mine eating pickles."

"Werecats aren't fond of pickles," said Gareth from the front passenger seat. "Or cucumbers in general. So, I don't think our child will like them, either."

Cyn knew that when Gareth used "our" he was referring collectively to him, Thomas, and Angela. It might've been Gareth who impregnated his mate, but the baby was the progeny of all three. Cyn would never be able to have children. She was a vampire, like Thomas, but even if she were human again, Kane and Aris were infertile. It was why they had never mated with one of their own kind. She would never give birth to a child and, for a quick second, she felt a tiny pang of jealousy. She put those useless feelings away. She'd be the best aunt ever to the little one and enjoy mommyhood vicariously through Angela.

"We're here," announced Thomas as the SUV bounced along the pitted dirt road.

Cyn looked at the side window. Had these people never heard of paved roads? As she examined the town, she realized Hellion Hill was too small and isolated to merit a blacktop. Hell, there wasn't even a stoplight, just one lone four-way stop.

While it was late afternoon and the sun was unimpeded by clouds, Cyn wasn't worried. The myth of vampires going poof in sunlight wasn't exactly true. Most could tolerate indirect UV rays, and a little sunblock went a long way to prevent skin burning when a vampire was exposed to a full-on blast of sunlight. Not only could Cyn hang out in the daytime hours without any real consequences, but she could also see herself in mirrors, thank you very much. But other aspects, a blood diet, susceptibility to pure silver, and being warded off by garlic—all that shit was true.

"How did you find this place again, Thomas?" asked Cyn.

"He used Google to search for creepy towns no one wants to visit," teased Angela.

"Close," said Thomas. "Reese Valiant."

"Oo-wee. Reese Valiant, the Fire Pack alpha." Angela turned around and grinned at Cyn. "He's hotter than Saturday night barbecue."

Cyn laughed. "I see your hormones are revved to maximum."

"Anyway," continued Thomas, "he told me about this place. He said it's been a while since he's been here, but said it was so out-of-the-way no one could find us. At least, not easily."

"Did he mention it was completely abandoned?" asked Aris as he grimly looked out the window.

"No." Thomas pulled into a parking spot in front of a brick building with the sign: Winslow Bed and Breakfast. Gareth hopped out, opened the sliding door, and helped Angela out of the vehicle. Cyn, Aris, and Kane followed. They all met on the plank sidewalk.

The town had obviously been built in the 1800s, one of

many places established when this area experienced a gold rush. It looked like the set of a western movie, but it had the creepy feel of a horror flick. The wind blew, scattering leaves across the pitted road. The air was thick with a coppery scent that Cyn knew well. Blood. But it was old, the remnants of deaths long past.

Cyn shook her head, her skin vibrating with apprehension. "Valiant sent us to a freaking ghost town." People she could fight and kill, but spirits were another story.

"What happened here?" asked Angela, pointing to the large dark red stains on the plank sidewalk.

"Maybe there was a shoot-out at high noon," said Cyn. "And those were the losers."

"Tristan said Hellion Hill was occupied by humans when he visited."

"Half a century ago," reminded Gareth. "This place hasn't been occupied for a while."

"Yeah," said Angela, rubbing her arms. "The only occupants now are the kind that jump out at you and scream boo."

"Ghosts aren't real," said Aris confidently.

Cyn lifted an eyebrow. "Said the werecougar who is hanging out with vampires. And we know the Hunter is real, don't we?"

"The protector of the Valiant werecat colony isn't a ghost." Aris thought for a moment. "It's a ... thingie."

"Thingie." Cyn laughed and punched her mate on the arm. "You mean it's the ghost of a long dead being."

"The Hunter is not a ghost," insisted Aris.

Kane gripped his friend's shoulder. "Ghosts or not, it'll be dark soon and we need to settle in somewhere."

"Let's check in to the Winslow," said Thomas. "I'm pretty

sure they have rooms available." He opened the glass-paned door. Its ominous creak sent a chill through Cyn. Hellion Hill gave her the serious creeps. In fact, something very close to fear trembled inside her—and she wasn't afraid of much.

"We should do a perimeter search," said Kane. Kane was the older of Cyn's two mates and had once been part of those who guarded the Harper werecat colony. When they met, all three of them were sent on missions to kill Thomas, Angela, and Gareth. But everything changed when she died —thanks to her weak human heart—and she was turned into a bloodsucker. Now, here she was on the run with the people who used to be her targets but had become her family.

Shaking off the alpha of the Harper colony, Craig Harper, and the pissed-off vampire Eliza DuChamp, had not been easy. For the last two months, they'd stayed one step ahead of the deadly duo, hah, but eventually, they would need to face down their enemies. However, they couldn't keep moving place to place with a new baby. They all needed stability and safety, and that was especially true of the impending child. Cyn remembered too well traveling with her assassin father, learning the tricks of the death trade. She never went to school, never made friends, never did anything for the sheer joy of it. She only cared about the wet work until her heart decided to fail.

It was then she'd realized she'd had nothing. No one. Except for the promise of an evil vampire bitch to give her eternal life, she'd had very little to live for. But now? She had Aris and Kane, her spectacular werecat mates, and she had friends. True friends who understood loyalty and sacrifice.

"Cyn?" Aris's soft voice interrupted her thoughts. She

realized she was standing on the porch between Aris and Kane. The others had gone inside the hotel. "Are you all right?"

"Yeah. Just got lost on Memory Lane."

Aris kissed her and then Kane did, too. As usual, lust flared hot and bright in her belly. Oh, the things these men did to her. And the things she could do to them. Yummy. But now wasn't the time or place for a sweaty, awesome were-cougar sandwich.

"Rain check," said Kane, guessing at her thoughts.

Cyn smiled. The love and passion of these two men, her beautiful mates, awed her every day. She loved them both with her whole undead heart.

"There's something off about this place," said Kane. "I think we should make sure we're the only ones here."

Aris and Kane kissed Cyn again, more chaste this time. "Let's go," said Aris.

~

"Where are they?" screamed Eliza DuChamp. She punched the nearest wall, instantly crumbling the plaster and leaving a hole big enough to see the garden outside of the cottage. The smell of wet grass and dying roses filtered into the living room. It had rained earlier, leaving the night air cool and crisp.

Craig Harper rolled his eyes. Eliza was prone to fits of rage. He found her drama queen antics exhausting, but for now, he would tolerate the vampire's outbursts. He needed her to find his asshole half-brother and the human bitch who carried the mongrel, not to mention the two betrayers Aris and Kane. Eliza wanted the head, quite literally, of Thomas Moore and that of the assassin Cyn Salais, who had been sent to kill Thomas but, instead, had joined him.

What a clusterfuck.

Eliza had been the one to show up at his door and give him the news that not only did his brother and the mother of his brother's babe live, but also that they had the protection of Aris and Kane. Craig hadn't been able to father an heir yet, and the lack of a direct descendent made him look weak. He had three mates, damn it, and not one of them had gotten pregnant. Gareth and that half-breed child were the only threats to Craig's leadership. Instead of celebrating his secured position as alpha, he was chasing six people across the United States, and it pissed him off.

Craig studied the new hole in the wall. It wasn't like this place belonged to him. They were in one of the vampire's safe houses. Apparently, she kept them all over the world. She could access the basement to sleep during the day when she wasn't at her full strength. He'd been thinking of tossing her into the garden as the sun reached its zenith then staking her through the heart. For all her dramatics and childish temper tantrums, though, Eliza was incredibly dangerous and would most likely survive the attack long enough to kill him back. Thus, she was better to have as a friend not an enemy.

"You really need to stop destroying shit," he said mildly. "You won't have much of a safe house left if you keep punching out the walls."

Fury temporarily sated, Eliza shrugged. "I have minions." She flicked her wrist. "They can fix it."

To Eliza, humans were food, pets, and slaves. She could care less about their lives. They were toys to her. She broke and discarded them without remorse.

Craig had no love for humans but he ignored them.

They were inconsequential ants, after all. He didn't understand Eliza's pleasure in torturing those who'd done no wrong to her. But who was he to question the vampire's sickening proclivities? As soon as they tracked down and killed their targets, Craig would part company with Eliza and return to his colony, the triumphant leader, and he would have to see the mad bitch ever again. With Gareth dead, any hopes the rebel factions had to replace Craig would be gone.

"Did you contact the Alpha of the Valiant colony?" she asked.

"Yes. He claims to know nothing about Gareth and his friends." Craig snorted. "Not that Reese Valiant would tell me shit."

"I sense a history there." Despite her comment, Eliza didn't seem particularly interested in the answer.

Craig responded anyway. "We've had a few run-ins." And Craig had come out the loser every time. If he thought he could get away with it, he'd kill every werewolf in Valiant's territory and burn it every last bit of it to the ground. Craig rubbed the back of his neck as a tension headache began to throb. Taking down the Fire Pack alpha was a dream for another day. Now, he needed to crush his half-brother and all of his companions.

Eliza sashayed into the kitchen and opened a bottle of blood wine. Craig grimaced. Vampires and their blood diets made his stomach turn. And Eliza wasn't a delicate drinker. She guzzled, not caring when blood dribbled down her chin and neck. Disgusting.

"What if you contacted the Fire Pack alpha?" asked Craig.

"You think you have problems with that man? Thomas has the alpha's loyalty. Besides, vampires haven't lived near his territory in at least a century. The werewolves viciously routed them out. Aren't shifters your thing, anyway?"

"I don't lower myself to mixing with wild dogs."

Eliza laughed. "I think you have more enemies than I do. And that's quite an accomplishment." She poured the ruby red liquid into a wine glass and lifted it in a toast. "To killing those who have wronged us."

bby Valiant raced across the dewy grass, hot on the tails of two small cougar kittens who squalled their protests. That old adage about cats not liking water? In the case of her shifter twins, bath time was the equivalent of medieval torture.

"Haven't you heard that you shouldn't chase after werecougars?" called out Abby's unhelpful husband, Reese, alpha of the Valiant colony. "They'll only run faster."

"That's werewolves and dogs," she yelled over her shoulder. "Cats have more civility."

Reese laughed. "Tell that to our sons."

"You could help, you know," she called out.

"And miss out on this home movie opportunity?"

"Are you serious?"

The two golden-furred kittens reached the back fence and each veered off in different directions. Abby stalled her progress and decided playing the game as a human put her at a disadvantage. She turned around and faced her husband. Yep. He had his smartphone out and was definitely filming the twins' shenanigans. "Do you want to record me getting naked and shifting?"

"Nope. You naked is for my eyes only." Reese tapped his phone screen and then lowered the device. "Proceed."

She laughed as she stripped off her sundress and panties. Then she crouched on all fours and shifted. Four legs were far better for chasing bath-avoiding cubs. She easily caught up to Finn, pouncing on him lightly. Her son flattened, mewling. With her mouth, she gently picked him up by the scruff and took the kitten to her husband.

"One down," he said.

Fain had taken shelter in an oak tree. He lay across a low limb, staring down at his mother, tail swishing. Abby roared the equivalent of "Get down here now, mister."

Fain did as his mother requested and jumped the four feet from the branch to the ground. Abby turned and walked to Reese, and Fain sullenly followed.

"You'd think we were trying to dip them in acid instead of soap and water." Reese scooped up his other son. "I'll get them into the tub."

Abby sat on her haunches and watched her husband take their children into the house. She yawned, resisting the urge to lie down and rest in the middle of the backyard. Raising werecougars was hard work. But she was grateful for her family—and gladly sacrificed sleep and, on occasion, sanity to have them. It was hard to believe that she'd once run as far from Reese as possible. When they'd met, she couldn't have his children—and the alpha had needed heirs. She'd called on the Hunter, the protector spirit of the Valiant colony, to take her life. She'd realize too late that she'd been incredibly stupid. Luckily, the Hunter was a compassionate being and had healed Abby's barren womb.

And now she had two beautiful boys with the man she loved most in the world.

She popped up onto all fours and loped toward her discarded clothes.

Before she'd gotten halfway across the yard, dark gray smoke appeared in front of her. The smoke swirled into a grandmotherly figure. The Hunter. She had silvery gray hair tucked into a bun, a wrinkled face that featured kindly brown eyes, and a plump, huggable body. She wore what some humans called "church clothes." Dress. Hose. Sensible flats. And a string of pearls around her neck.

"Abigail," said the Hunter. "How are you, dear?"

Abby answered with a short, happy sound.

"That's wonderful." She tilted her head. "Would you mind taking your human form so we can actually talk?"

Abby shifted. Dusk painted the sky purple. The wind picked up, but despite its gentle warmth, Abby felt a chill. Werecougars had no hang-ups about nudity, but even so, she felt vulnerable standing before an ancient spirit in just her birthday suit. "Let me get dressed."

She hurriedly put on her panties and the green summer frock. The Hunter wasn't known for casual visitations. In fact, until Abby had called on her nearly two years ago, the Hunter hadn't been seen in the Valiant colony for at least a generation.

Suddenly anxious, Abby asked, "Why are you here?" She huffed out a breath. "I'm sorry. That was rude. It's nice to see you again." She paused, foreboding twisting her stomach. "Is anything wrong?"

"I've come to warn you of the impending apocalypse."

"What?"

"No need to soil yourself. I'm kidding."

"You're hilarious," said Abby drolly. She rubbed her

belly, trying to unknot the tension coiled there. "So you're just here for a social call?"

The Hunter put her hands on her plump hips. "What if I am? Why does something have to be wrong for me to show up?"

Abby lifted an eyebrow. "Because you're the protector spirit of the Valiant colony, and you're scary as hell."

"Well, there's that." The Hunter sighed. "All right. I'm here because I need your help."

"My help?" Abby blinked at her. She couldn't imagine any scenario where a supernatural immortal being would need help with anything. Even so, she wasn't going to turn down any request because she owed the Hunter everything. The woman had given her the greatest miracle ever. "What can I do, Hunter?"

"You know, I really don't like that name. Call me Judith."

"Your name is Judith?" Disbelief coated Abby's words.

"No. My real name is irrelevant. I like being a Judith."

"Okay dokay. Judith, it is."

"Thank you." Judith's wrinkled face lit up with a wide, satisfied smile. "Now, where's that husband of yours?"

"Bathing two very reluctant boys, who will soon be clean and in their jammies, waiting for a bedtime story."

"Oh! Can I tell them a story?"

"Does it involve mutilation, murder, and mayhem?"

"The best stories do," said Judith. "I could tell them about the battle between the Valiant shifters and the Ladon. It's on my mind because the Ladon is why I'm here."

"No." Abby crossed her arms. What the hell was a Ladon? "I'd rather my children not have nightmares. You can read them The Cougars Go to Town."

Judith looked supremely disappointed. "Does anyone die in this tale?"

"Nope." Abby linked her arm around Judith's, and they headed toward the house.

I t sensed the presence of others. In the damp, dark cave the Ladon lifted its scaly head and took in the scents filtering into its home. Ah, the robust scent of sweat. It knew well the delicious aroma of human. It flickered its tongue, tasting the air. Only one? The others were ... not human. Two were dead. It hissed in disgust. Dead things didn't make good meals.

It inhaled once more.

This smell was a familiar one. One that it feared.

Cat creatures.

It bobbed its head, slithering to the entrance of the cave.

It examined the forest, checking for signs of the intruders. Satisfied the newcomers were not near its hiding place, it returned to the darkest part of the cave.

The hole was ten feet across, barely large enough to contain its massive size. It was closer than ever to its treasure —to its revenge.

It had taken decades to find the only thing that would kill its enemy and its terrible shifter offspring. It would not make the same mistake as it had two centuries before, when the Valiant shifters had nearly killed it. After the Ladon had healed from its near fatal wounds, it had searched the continent for the Valiant heart. It had been hidden well.

But the Ladon was closer than ever to uncovering the heart. It could feel the pulse, the warmth, the magic.

It turned and weaved back toward the entrance of the cave. Whoever entered the town could never leave, not without the Ladon removing the boundary spell. It could hunt these new arrivals at its leisure.

I n his cougar form, Aris padded into the copse of trees. It was a private spot in the otherwise dense woods. He stopped, rolled onto his back, and looked up at the velvet tapestry of the night sky. Other than a few more bloodstains from old deaths, he hadn't found anything untoward lurking around Hellion Hill.

Nearby, he heard Kane's yowl and he answered it. A minute later, werecougar Kane loped into the small clearing, stopping when he got to Aris.

"Boys," said Cyn as she arrived. "I got nada. I think whatever happened here—and whatever did it—is long gone."

Aris shifted into his human form. "I didn't find anything, either."

Cyn strode toward him, her gaze heated as she took in his nakedness. Unlike her shifter men who were unaffected by nudity most of the time, she was not so immune, especially when it came to her two hunky mates. She was a lucky, lucky girl.

Cyn melted into Aris' arms, and he kissed her. Hard. Her body responded instantly to the heat of his mouth and the hard cock pressing against her sex.

One of the perks of being a vampire was increased speed and strength. Cyn discarded her clothing in 1.2 seconds. In the meanwhile, Kane had reverted to his human form.

Huzzah! Time for her sweaty, awesome werecougar sandwich.

She faced Kane while Aris stood behind her. The men began to touch her. Oh, they knew all the right places. Aris kissed the sensitive spot behind her ear while Kane cupped her breast and rubbed his thumbs across her hardened nipples.

She shuddered.

In the next second, Kane scooped her into his arms and gently put her on the ground, lying on her left side. Aris laid down on her right. Both men skimmed their palms down her ribs, long, warm fingers drifting across her thighs.

Her flesh contracted from the light contact—and made electric need zap every cell in her body.

Aris was his usual impatient self. He kissed her aggressively, plundering her mouth with his tongue and nipping at her lips. She cupped his face and his ferocity with her own. Meanwhile, Kane parted the wet folds of her sex and stroked her sensitive clit.

She moaned.

"My turn," growled Kane.

Cyn rolled toward Kane and met his mouth with hers while Aris kissed her shoulders and stroked her flesh.

She reached down and gripped Kane's shaft, eliciting a groan. Aris pressed against her, his cock hard against her buttocks. His fingers skimmed her hip and found her slick sex.

Her excitement ratcheted up another notch.

She pressed against Aris, her back against the firm muscles of his chest, while Kane nipped at her flesh. Her nails dug into Kane's broad shoulders.

"That feels so good," she murmured.

Aris' fingers tangled into her hair, tugging lightly. Kane took advantage of her bared throat, trailing kisses up her neck until he reached her lips. As he conquered her mouth, heated passion streaked her.

"God, you're wet," said Kane as he slipped his hand

between them. He delved into her swollen pussy, sinking two fingers inside her while Aris continued to stroke her clit.

She moaned, floating on the river of pleasure created by her mates.

Cyn wrapped a leg around Kane, and he bent to suck on her distended nipples. She cried out as his tongue swirled around the sensitized peaks.

"I can't wait," she huffed. "Please. Please."

Holding Cyn in his arms, Aris rolled onto his back. He grasped her breasts, playing with her aching nipples as she lifted up her legs and held onto her thighs, opening herself to both of her mates. She guided Aris' cock inside her, shuddering as he filled her.

Kane kneeled between Aris' legs, waiting patiently as Aris thrusted. The first time they'd both taken her this way, she'd worried she wouldn't be able to accommodate their size, but she had. It was an ecstasy she had never before experienced.

"Oh, God," she moaned. Her pussy clenched around Aris' pumping erection.

"You make me so hot," whispered Aris. "I want you so much."

"Take me," said Kane hoarsely. "Take us both."

Aris stilled so that Kane could work his cock inside Cyn. Now, Kane's shaft lay on top of Aris'.

The double penetration stretched Cyn to the limit, and she loved it. She shuddered, her mates breathing heavy, as they adjusted to the new position.

Kane took the lead, slowly thrusting into her, his cock sliding against Aris' as he caught the rhythm. With two sizable shafts impaling her, and Cyn held on for dear life as her mates took her fully.

"You're so wet," muttered Kane,

"And tight," said Aris.

The dual rhythm took her to the edge of ecstasy.

Aris tugged her nipples and sharp pleasure arced, contracting her womb.

"I'm going to come," said Kane.

Aris groaned, and Cyn knew he was close to coming, too.

Kane's hands gripped Cyn's thighs, his face, a mask of pleasure.

"I can't wait," she said, panting. "Oh, God."

She cried out as she orgasmed, waves of bliss enrobing her entire being. Kane moaned, still embedded deeply inside her as he jettisoned his seed.

Aris followed seconds later, arching up as he squeezed her breasts and shuddered with his own release.

Kane removed his softening erection and collapsed to the ground. Cyn wiggled free of Aris and rolled off, stretching out between her mates. Both men turned onto their sides and scooted in close, hugging her tightly.

"Cat snuggles are the best," she teased. Then she sobered. "I love you both so much."

"We love you, too," said Aris.

"Forever," added Kane.

3

"I was once the alpha," said Judith. "Two hundred years ago."

Reese finished pouring the coffee and paused, his gaze on the Hunter ... er, Judith. "You were a werecougar?"

"Yes. We were settled here before the Europeans came to the shores of America. The surrounding Native American tribes had legends about us." She paused and gave both Abby and Reese a direct look. "Do you really want to hear about how the original shifters traveled from the wilds of Canada to make a home here?"

"Maybe not now," Abby admitted. She added cream to her coffee. "But it is a story I'd like to hear one day."

Reese returned the carafe to the coffee maker and then sat down at the dining room table with his mate and the Valiant colony protector. He stared at the grandmotherly figure of Judith, trying to reconcile the image with the gangly, terrifying creature that had originally presented itself to him and his mate. The Hunter was not at all what he expected.

"I often clashed with my brother. He was younger, but as

a male, he felt entitled to be the alpha. I don't know what it is about having a penis that makes the male species feel so superior to us."

Abby snorted into her coffee mug. Reese glanced at her, brows raised.

"Oh, I know you don't feel that way, Reese," added Judith. "We are entering more enlightened times, thank goodness." She looked down into the mug. "What is this?"

"Coffee."

She sniffed it and then turned to Abby. "Why does yours smell different?"

"Because I use flavored creamer."

"Ah." Judith took a sip and grimaced. "This tastes like dirt off a coyote's butt."

Abby laughed. "It's interesting you know what butt dirt tastes like," she teased. She took the creamer container and stirred a generous amount into Judith's mug. "Try it now."

Judith glanced at the cup warily, but took another sip. She smiled. "That's far better."

Reese couldn't believe he was sitting in his house with the Hunter—the feared protector spirit of the Valiants—and acting like it was the most normal thing in the world.

Life could be really weird.

"Back to the topic at hand," said Judith. "My brother, let's call him Assface, shall we?"

Reese swallowed a laugh, and he could see that his wife was doing the same.

"Assface decided he'd rather see me dead than lead our colony." She sighed. "It was then that he called the creature forth—the Ladon. Our people fought bravely. The Ladon took many lives, including my mate's. I admit that my grief was nearly more than I could handle. But my rage—well, that was brighter still."

Reese watched his wife squeeze Judith's hand, her empathy palpable.

Judith smiled. "I went our shaman, and told him I wanted to annihilate Assface. And I didn't care about the cost.

"He gathered shamans from other colonies to create the spell that would give me the power to defeat my brother and the Ladon. But such power comes at a price. I gave up the afterlife, and the chance of ever seeing my mate again, for my vengeance. The shamans separated me from my spiritual heart—a failsafe if my transformation took my sanity. They hid it, as well they could. It's my only vulnerability. Anyway, the form of my vengeance was this one." She looked down. "Well, not this one exactly. I became spirit with the ability to shapeshift into anything. I became the protector of the Valiant colony.

"By the way, Valiant was my idea." She patted Reese's hand. "That's how I thought of my mate. Valiant. So that was the name I gave my son, who became alpha."

"Wait." Reese felt his heart turn over in his chest. "If you gave your son the Valiant name then I'm related to you?"

"Duh," said Judith. "I'm your direct ancestor. Why else would I answer the call of your mate?"

"But ... but ... what about the other times you were called upon?"

"I help the Valiants. Sometimes the way to do that is to help those close to you. This is all irrelevant, Reese. The important thing to know now is that I killed my brother and with him, the evil he carried. I thought I had rid the earth of the Ladon, too. But apparently it slithered away to heal."

"Where is it now?" asked Abby.

"Near a place called Hellion Hill." Judith gripped her mug. "And it's found my heart."

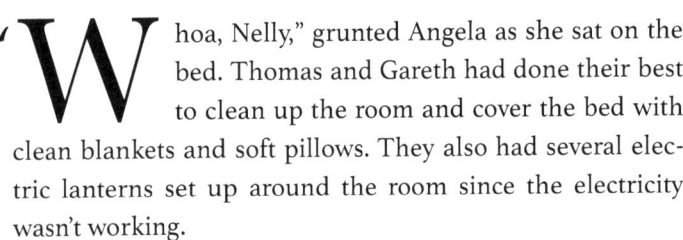

"Whoa, Nelly," grunted Angela as she sat on the bed. Thomas and Gareth had done their best to clean up the room and cover the bed with clean blankets and soft pillows. They also had several electric lanterns set up around the room since the electricity wasn't working.

Thomas helped her lie down. He took off her shoes and rubbed her feet. Worry crowded his chest as he stared at Angela.

She gasped, her expression filled with pain. She breathed through the contraction. "Would you stop looking at me like that?" she asked. "You act like I'm dying."

Gareth entered the room with a wet cloth. "The water's working." He leaned over and placed it on Angela's forehead.

"Oh, that feels good. Why is it so hot in here?"

Thomas shared a look with Gareth, whose countenance revealed the werecougar's fear for their mate.

Angela hissed as she grabbed her middle. "Goddamn it. This fucking hurts."

Thomas placed his hands on Angela's belly. Their son's heart beat strongly. He had turned, head down toward the birth canal. Angela's abdomen seized under his hands. The contraction was strong. Too strong for the beginning of labor. At least, that's what the books had said.

"The contractions are a minute apart," he said, looking up at Gareth.

"That can't be right. Braxton-Hicks?"

"Fuck that," said Angela, panting. "This is the real deal, trust me."

"What's going on?" asked Cyn. She and the two other werecougars stood in the doorway.

"She's going into labor," answered Gareth, his voice verging on panic. "Call Reese. He'll bring his colony's midwife to us."

"Cell phones don't work here," said Kane.

"We'll drive to the Valiant colony." Cyn looked at Thomas, her expression reflecting his own concern. "It's just a couple of hours, right?"

"Round trip will be at least four hours. I don't think we have that kind of time." Thomas feared for his mate. Angela looked exceptionally pale.

"Let's go down the road, out of the woods and try to call Reese there," suggested Aris. "The dead zone can't reach that far."

"If that doesn't work," said Cyn, "we'll head to the nearest hospital and kidnap a doctor."

"You can't do that," Angela huffed.

"Yes, I can, sweets. It's kinda my specialty. You hang in there." Cyn and her mates left.

Thomas heard the car doors open and shut and the engine rev. The spinning tires spit gravel and squealed against the pitted road as the mini-van took off.

Gareth was trying to help Angela with the breathing exercises they had all practiced.

It wasn't going well.

"Why didn't we get morphine?" she wailed. Sweat dripped down her face. "I'd really like some morphine."

"It's okay," soothed Gareth.

"The hell it is!"

Gareth looked at Thomas helplessly. He had the ability to lessen her pain, but Angela wouldn't hear of it. She insisted on having the baby completely natural. And she also refused Thomas' offer to make her forget the labor process. It's part of being a mother, she'd said. He wouldn't go against her wishes, though he badly wanted to end her agony.

Angela screamed as another contraction viciously gripped her womb.

Thomas watched water spill out from between her thighs. In horror, he looked at the soaked bed. "Gareth, her amniotic sac broke."

The argument about who should stay and who should go was short. Mostly because Abby's stubborn mate knew he didn't have a chance in hell at convincing her to stay home. Abby wasn't letting her husband go off and battle the Ladon without her. Abby's parents were babysitting the twins, who were conked out for the night anyway. If things went well, she and Reese would be back before dawn broke.

The black SUV sat in the driveway, engine rumbling. It was early evening, but the sun had gone down leaving only the velvet black of night. The Hunter had insisted that their mission rely on only a few trusted members of the Valiant colony. That was easy enough—all five of Abby's brothers were guardians of the colony in general and the alpha in particular.

Abby sat in the passenger seat of the SUV, and her husband on the driver's side. The Hunter sat in the back, marveling at the luxurious interior. Her brothers had squeezed into the seats behind the Hunter. Luckily the SUV was an extended cab.

"I need one of these," said Judith, patting the leather seats.

"Well, they're not as fast as you are for transporting," said Thomas as he put the car into drive. "It'll take a good two hours just to get to Hellion Hill."

"Oh, that's not fast enough at all." She waved at hand at the engine. The SUV revved into high gear and shot down the road. "We should be there in less than thirty now."

"I can't drive this thing!" yelled Reese.

"You don't have to," said Judith. "I'm driving it."

"From the backseat?" he asked, horror in his voice. Abby watched Reese grip the useless steering wheel so hard his knuckles turned white. As they zoomed past other cars and weaved between the slower the ones, Abby felt her stomach pitch.

"Are you sure you know what you're doing?" she asked Judith.

"Of course I do." Judith smiled winsomely. "Magical spirit, remember?"

＊

Eliza DuChamp held up her smartphone, a smirk twisting her lips. She stood in the safe house kitchen having just finished off the blood wine. "I found them." She looked at Craig, who was the epitome of an asshole. He lounged on the couch, perfecting an air of boredom. "They're in a place called Hellion Hill."

"Are you sure?"

"Yes. I have eyes and ears everywhere. My humans know that if that if they lie to me or fail me, I will suck them dry." She rubbed her tongue over her fangs. That blood wine, delicious as it was, had not been enough sustenance.

"How long will it take to get this Hellion Hill place?"

Craig stood up from the couch. Eliza had to admit that the werecougar alpha had quite the outer package. If she didn't loathe him, she might well seduce him. But the shifter cat had made it clear how distasteful he found her. His revulsion angered her to no end. She was beautiful and powerful and wealthy. He was nothing compared to her.

"That's a bit of good news. It's less than hour away. And by vampire? Mere minutes."

Craig grimaced. "I don't want to fly anywhere else with you."

"You are such a whiner." She threw her hands up. "Fine! I'll magic us there instead."

His eyes widened. "I thought transportation ability was a vampire myth."

"Not a myth. But only the oldest and most powerful can perform the magic needed."

"I still think we should take some of my guardians with me."

"Like that worked out so well for you before." She delighted in his pained look. The only reason Craig Harper had deigned to chase their prey himself is because the last time he sent minions, they'd betrayed him.

She, too, had been betrayed. Her rage for Thomas was a bright and hot as a star. How dare he dump her for a human? And Cyn Salais? Eliza sneered. She would eat that bitch's flesh and gnaw on her bones.

"We stick to our plan," she said. "No one else is needed. Agreed?"

"Yeah." Craig stuck his hands into his jean pockets. "So how do we do this transport shit?"

"Put your arms around me," she said. "Don't worry," she said, flashing fang, "I won't bite you."

"If you want to keep that lovely face intact, you won't," said Craig.

"Aw. You say the sweetest things." Eliza enacted the transportation magic and in the next instant, they stood among pine trees, the night sky barely visible above them.

Craig stepped out of Eliza's embrace, and looked around. "Are they hiding in the trees?"

"Don't be an idiot. The town is that way," she said. "I wasn't going to plop us in the middle of street. Sheesh."

"Wait. What is that?"

Eliza tilted her head and listened. "It sounds like hissing."

The ground beneath their feet shook, and the next thing Eliza saw was a building-sized serpent crash through the pines. Before she knew what was happening, the huge triangular head dove at them.

The serpent snapped Craig up with its powerful jaws. Eliza heard the sickening crunch of bones and then the shifter was swallowed. In horror, she watched the lump that used to be Craig worked its way down the creature's throat.

She turned and ran. Panic clouded her thoughts and slowed her limbs. She had never felt this terrified in her life. She raised her arms and lifted into the air, intending to fly as far away as she could.

Too little, too late. The snake caught her by the legs and threw her to the ground. The last thing Eliza saw was the huge curved fangs, dripping with Craig's blood, descend upon her.

4

Just as Cyn hit the "You're Now Leaving Hellion Hill" sign, the mini-van went kaput. She slammed on the brakes and shifted into park. "What the fuck?"

"The last thing we need is broken-down car," said Kane as he and Aris jumped out. Cyn popped the hood. Worry beat in her undead heart. Angela had not looked good. Her skin was ashen—and the pain in her expression struck fear into Cyn. Surely Angela wouldn't die. *I won't let that happen.*

"There's nothing wrong," called out Kane.

"Come out here, Cyn," yelled Aris.

Cyn exited the car. At this altitude, the night air felt chilly. The stars were pinpricks in the sky's dark tapestry. If she wasn't in the middle of a crisis, she might actually enjoy the scenery. Kane and Aris stood in the middle of the road.

"Watch this." Aris stepped forward, and he immediately stumbled back as though he'd hit a trampoline. Kane tried next with the same bouncy results. Cyn walked forward and felt like she'd run into invisible gelatin.

"What is this?" she asked.

"It's a magical border." Kane shook his head. "Damn it." He turned to Cyn. "We can't leave."

"Well, that's just fucking great!" A loud hissing erupted. Cyn went to the minivan and kicked the tire. "Fuck you, you fucking fucker."

"It's not the car." Aris pointed toward the dense woods to the left of the road.

Cyn paused, tilting her head. Her vampire senses were still fairly new to her, so she wasn't yet relying on them too heavily. She concentrated on the odd noise and realized the loud rasping was definitely coming from the nearby forest. The trees wobbled and limbs cracked as whatever was hissing made its way toward them.

The next thing she saw was the biggest goddamned snake she'd ever laid eyes on. The serpent was a brilliant red with a triangular head as a big as Volvo, and its scaly body as wide as a freeway. Its yellow eyes with diamond irises examined them coldly.

"I hate snakes," said Aris.

"I'm not too fond of them, either," said Cyn. "But I think we're looking at the thing that killed everyone in town."

The serpent's tail appeared and whipped down onto the minivan, flattening it so hard the tires blew out.

"Holy shit," cried Cyn. She backed away, her gaze on the swaying monster as it lifted its tail once more.

"Angela's too vulnerable right now. We have to lead it away from town," yelled Kane. "C'mon." He turned and ran into the woods on the opposite side of the road. Aris and Cyn followed.

And so did the snake from hell.

～

Angela screamed. Her hand gripped Gareth's so tightly, he thought she might cut off the circulation. It had been fifteen minutes, and other than her agony visibly growing stronger with every contraction, she hadn't progressed very much.

His mate went limp against the pillows. She'd been passing out between contractions. He was certain that wasn't normal.

"Shouldn't the baby at least be crowning now?" Gareth asked.

"I don't know." Thomas looked worriedly at Angela. "It was stupid to bring her here."

"We weren't planning on staying that long. And we couldn't risk her life or our child's by getting caught. With Eliza and Craig working together, we're barely staying ahead of them."

"You're right. It's just ... her heartbeat is erratic. But the baby's heartbeat is even and strong."

Angela awoke. Gareth helped her sit up as another ribbon of pain squeezed her belly. He hated that he could not alleviate her agony.

"This sucks," she said in a hoarse whisper. Her eyes fluttered closed, and she went limp once more.

"Help her," said Gareth.

"I don't know what to do. The books didn't prepare us for this."

"Alleviate her pain, Thomas."

He shook his head. "I promised her." Gareth could feel his friend's helplessness—he felt exactly the same.

They heard tires skid across gravel. Relief cascaded through Gareth. The return of his friends surely meant they'd found help. At the very least, Cyn could offer womanly advice about the situation.

"Thank the goddess," said Thomas.

Doors opened and feet stomped on the plank sidewalk. Gareth rushed to the door and yelled downstairs, "Hurry up, damn it!"

He returned to Angela just in time for her to awaken and begin screaming.

"What the hell is going?" asked an unfamiliar male voice.

Gareth looked up to find Reese, his mate Abby, an elderly woman, and five huge men crowded in the doorway. "Reese? What are you doing here?"

"I'm here—wait a minute. Why are y'all here?"

"Oh, my God. Who cares?" The grandmother hurried into the room. "Abby, help me."

"She needs to be in a squatting position, not laid out like a wet noodle on the bed," berated the older woman. "Gravity will help her, you idiots."

"Who the hell are you?" asked Gareth.

"Judith. Now move."

Gareth shared a stunned look with Thomas as Judith and Abby muscled them out of the way. "She needs support." Judith glared at the men. "That's you two. Get on either side of her. Pretend you're chairs, for heaven's sake."

Gareth did as the lady demanded. They put Angela's arms around their necks as directed and held their mate under her thighs. Gareth glanced at the doorway. Reese still stood there, but the five men had disappeared. Good. Angela already had too big of an audience.

"What happened to your minivan?" asked Reese.

Gareth felt the breath whoosh out of him. "What do you mean?"

"It looks like a pancake."

"No doubt the Ladon did that," said Judith as she shoved covers underneath Angela.

"What the fuck is a Ladon?" snapped Thomas.

Angela screamed—cutting short the conversation. Judith kneeled in front of her and gently felt between her bloodied thighs. "I can feel the baby's head. Excellent."

"Our friends took the minivan," said Gareth. "Aris, Kane, and Cyn."

"No one was in the car," said Reese. "We checked. I'll take my guardians and search for your friends." The Valiant alpha's face looked relieved to have the excuse to leave the room.

"And don't forget to kill the Ladon," directed Judith.

"That's the first thing on my to-do list," promised Reese. He glanced at his wife. "I'll be back."

"You better," she said.

With Cyn's vampire strength and speed, she easily kept up with her mates, both of whom had taken on their cougar forms. The ugly, persistent snake slithered right behind them, knocking aside trees like they were matchsticks. The woods had thinned out considerably. They ran across a field of tall grass, headed toward a large, stony outcropping. At the bottom, she saw the entrance to a cave. Either they scaled the craggy rock and attempted to hide in that cave, or they would have to turn and fight. She knew which option she preferred.

"We're far enough away from town," said Cyn. "It's time to kill this thing."

She slid to a stop and turned, drawing silver half-sword from its hip holster. She left the gun on her other hip. She didn't think bullets would penetrate the serpent's thick scales, but the pure silver sword caused damage on most supernatural creatures. She hoped it would work on super strong, ginormous snakes.

Her mates roared as they crouched by her side, long golden tails swishing.

The snake slithered into the clearing, its forked tongue flickering as it coiled the back of its body. The front part rose into the air, towering above them.

Cyn let out a war cry, hoisting her sword as she ran toward the beast. Her mates followed, roaring their own battle songs.

The sword easily pierced the scales and Cyn twisted the blade, causing the creature to screech in pain. Aris and Kane dug in with their claws and teeth. Cyn pulled the sword out and struck again and again.

The serpent shook its massive body, easily dislodging them. All three went flying backward. Cyn landed hard on her backside, but as a vampire, she wasn't hurt easily. Within seconds, Cyn was up and charging the beast again.

Her goddamned sword was still embedded in the monster's flesh.

"Need help?" called out a voice.

"You think?" she screamed back, not caring who'd arrived, as long as they were on her side.

Five huge cougars slunk out of the tree line, growling as they approached the serpent. Cyn wrenched her sword free.

"I'm Reese," said the man as he approached.

"I don't give a fuck who you are as long as you help us kill this thing."

Reese grinned. And then he got on all fours and shifted, his clothes shredding as he took on his werecougar form.

The snake reared back, trying to uncoil and slither away. But now there were eight pissed-off cougars and one furious vampire attacking it. It bobbed its head and undulated its body, hissing and screeching as the cats dug in claws and teeth, slashing and biting.

Cyn decided the only way to end this bullshit was to put her sword through its braincase. She jumped onto the back of the serpent, digging her fingers in-between the scales and climbing the moving snake tower.

She looked down at the mauling cougars. Despite the snake's best efforts to rid itself of the attacking cats, it couldn't shake them. Cyn reached the top without sweating or huffing—yay for being a vampire!

When she got to the top of the beast's head, she drew her sword from its scabbard. Holding on to one of the scales, she lifted the sword and jammed it as hard as she could into its skull. "Die, motherfucker."

The snake screeched as blood spurted out of its mouth.

It swayed heavily and then began to fall.

Cyn jumped and landed on her feet, other than a few scratches, none the worse for wear. The monster slammed into the ground, gurgling. Not one to leave a target still breathing, Cyn used her sword and her vampire strength to saw off its head.

When she was through, she was soaked in its pungent blood, and the ground was covered in flesh and innards. Wait a minute. She looked again at the mess on the ground and recognized the mutilated body of Eliza.

Kane and Aris padded up next to her and shifted into their human forms. "Who is that?"

"Eliza DuChamp. Ding, dong, the bitch is dead."

"And so is Craig. Look." Aris pointed at a bloodied lump.

Cyn realized she was looked at the severed head of a man. "Well, we killed three assholes with one sword."

"This is good news," said Kane.

"We'll celebrate later," said Aris.

Kane and Aris shifted back into cougars and joined the others waiting near the tree line.

Cyn joined them and looked down at herself. Whew. She looked bad and smelled wore. "I need to get dead snake off me—and fast. Angela still needs us."

ngela grunted. "I n-need to push."

"Not yet. Wait for your next contraction," directed Judith. "Then you can push."

The next band of pain came quickly. Angela gritted her teeth and bore down.

"Excellent," said Judith. "The head's through." She leaned forward and wiped the mucous from the baby's mouth. He responded with a loud wail. "One more push, dear. Get those shoulders through, and you're home free."

The next contraction came swiftly, and Angela screamed as she pushed down one last time. The baby slipped free, and Judith caught the newborn with practiced hands. "Lay her upright on the bed and stuff some pillows behind her head."

Gareth and Thomas obeyed. Angela looked utterly exhausted, but her smile was pure joy. Judith put the babe on Angela's belly.

"Hey there," she said in a soft voice. "Welcome, little one."

"Who's cutting the cord?" asked Judith. She held up a gleaming pair of gold scissors.

"Where did those come from?" exclaimed Thomas.

"Did I mention I was a magical spirit?" She held out the scissors. "Which daddy will it be?"

"We'll do it together," said Thomas.

The men, as one, held the scissors and cut the umbilical cord.

"Judith, maybe you can give the little guy a cleanup while I help Angela with the afterbirth?" Abby waved away the boys. "You go with her."

Gareth and Thomas did as they were told.

~

"Good news, people," said Cyn as she strolled into the room. "We've killed the snake, and we don't have to worry about vampire bitch and alpha asshole anymore."

"The Ladon apparently ate them," said Reese. "Helluva way to die. Couldn't happen to a nicer duo." He paused, looking at Gareth. "Sorry. I know Craig was your brother."

"Half-brother. And we were never close. I was a cub born to one of the alpha's mistresses—and I was never officially allowed into the royal family. Craig spent most of his life figuring out ways to torment me." Gareth leaned down and kissed the top of Angela's head. "This is all the family I need."

Angela looked up, her face one of contentment as her son suckled her breast, having his first meal. "Cyn, what happened to you? You're completely soaked."

"I had to jump in a lake and wash snake guts off me."

"It didn't help with the smell," said Thomas, his nose wrinkling.

"I didn't have any soap handy. Sheesh." Cyn looked at Angela. "When do I get some cuddle time with the little guy?"

"You are not holding this baby until you're clean," admonished Angela.

Aris and Kane put their arms around Cyn. "Don't worry," said Aris. "We'll make sure we soap her from head to toe."

"Squeaky clean," agreed Kane, grinning.

"Well!" said Judith. "Isn't this wonderful? The Ladon is no more, there's a new life in this world, and y'all have already started a community of mixed paranormal beings."

"What are you talking about, Hunter?" asked Reese.

"Hunter?" Kane looked taken aback. "You're *the* Hunter —the protector spirit of the Valiant Colony."

"Call me Judith." She lifted her hands up. "This town is deserted. It's hidden away, far from the humans. It's a perfect spot for supernatural beings to live."

"She has a point," mused Gareth.

"Craig is dead," said Thomas. "What about your colony, Gareth?"

"I've never been interested in being alpha of the Harper cats. Craig's manic pursuit of pure bloodlines is what drove me away to begin with. Let someone else take up the mantle."

"There is another reason—a favor, if you will, for you to settle here. Come, let me show you." Judith waved her hand. Thomas, Gareth, Reese, Cyn, Kane and Aris disappeared with her. She left Abby behind to stay with Angela and the baby.

In the blink of an eye, the seven of them arrived at the clearing where the Ladon lay massacred. Despite the darkness, everyone could see the carnage left by the dead serpent.

"Yuck," said Judith.

"Tell me about it," muttered Cyn.

"Into the cave, everyone." Judith led the way. Luckily, everyone had supernatural eyesight and found it easy to navigate in the dark. In the back part of the cave, they came upon a large hole. At its bottom, they saw a soft red glow.

"That's your heart?" asked Reese.

"Yes." She turned to them. "If I left here, with you all protecting it, I will be safe. And I can continue to protect the Valiants—and this new town of yours."

"I'm tired of running," said Cyn. "I'm all for settling down."

"The location makes it ideal—and easy to protect." Kane nodded. "What do the rest of you think?"

"Yes," said Thomas.

"I'm in," added Gareth.

Everyone looked at Aris. "Well, I'm not leaving," he said.

"Excellent. You are now bound to the Valiants, and to me, by pledging yourself to—what's the name of this place again?"

"Hellion Hill."

Judith grimaced. "That's a terrible name."

"How about Sanctuary?" asked Thomas.

"Much better. You have pledged your loyalty to the town of Sanctuary, and are now under my protection." She linked her arm around Reese's. "Let's get you and your home. Those babies of yours will be up soon."

"And we have a babe of our own to tend to," said Gareth.

"And a whole town to build," added Cyn. She smiled. "I think we're going to love this place."

ROMANCES BY MICHELE BARDSLEY

Broken Heart Paranormal Romances

#1 - I'm the Vampire, That's Why

#2 - Don't Talk Back to Your Vampire

#3 - Because Your Vampire Said So

#4 - Wait Till Your Vampire Gets Home

#5 - Over My Dead Body

#6 - Come Hell or High Water

#7 - Cross Your Heart

#8 - Must Love Lycans

#9 - Only Lycans Need Apply

#10 - Broken Heart Tails

#11 - Some Lycan Hot

#12 - You'll Understand When You're Dead

#13 - Lycan on the Edge

#14 - Your Lycan or Mine?

Lost Souls & Broken Hearts

A Broken Heart Paranormal Romance Spin-off

#1 - Amazing Grace

#2 - Peace in the Valley

#3 - How Great Thou Art

∾

Wizards of Nevermore Fantasy Romances

#1 - Never Again

#2 - Now or Never

The Pack Rules Shifter Romances

#1 - Alpha

#2 - Wolves

#3 - Bears

#4 - Dragons

#5 - Cats

Single Title Paranormal Romances

Holiday Bites

Blood Kiss

Cursed

Wired

Magical Acts

Tek

Single Title Contemporary Romances

Frisky Business

Mirrors Falls: Daddy in Training and Bride in Training

MYSTERIES BY MICHELE BARDSLEY

Violetta Graves Paranormal Mysteries

The Complete Series

#1 - In Good Spirits

#2 - A Spirited Defense

#3 - Getting in the Spirit

#4 - Plagued by Spirits

#5 - Free Spirit

Graves Detective Agency Cozy Mysteries

#1 - A Grave Mistake (December 2019)

#2 - One Foot in the Grave (April 2019)

#3 - Grave Robber (June 2019)

#4 - Take It to the Grave (October 2019)

#5 - Grave Stone (January 2020)

Broken Heart Paranormal Cozy Mysteries

#1 - Dirty Rotten Vampires (October 2018)

#2 - Twelve Angry Vampires (January 2019)

#3 - Citizen Vampire (April 2019)

#4 - The Vampire Connection (August 2019)

#5 - A Vampire in Paris (October 2019)

≈

Garden Grove Witches of the Northwest

#1 - A Witch in Thyme (November 2018)

#2 - Stop and Spell the Roses (February 2019)

#3 - Every Witch Has Her Thorn (May 2019)

#4 - Spells Get Better With Sage (August 2019)

#5 - Witch Hazel Are You? (November 2019)

Antique Shop Cozy Mysteries

#1 - The Case of the Caretaker's Curios (December 2019)

#2 - The Case of the Ballerina's Bauble (March 2019)

#3 - The Case of the Tyrant's Treasure (July 2019)

#4 - The Case of the Actor's Artwork (September 2019)

#5 - The Case of the Widow's Watch (December 2019)

ABOUT THE AUTHOR

Michele Bardsley is a *New York Times* and *USA Today* best-selling author of paranormal fiction. When she's not writing tales of otherworldly adventures, she consumes chocolate, crochets hats, reads voraciously, and spends time with her Viking hubby and their fur babies.

Visit Michele's Website
http://www.michelebardsley.com

Subscribe to Michele's Newsletter
http://www.michelebardsleynewsletter.com

facebook.com/MicheleBardsleyNovels

bookbub.com/authors/michele-bardsley

goodreads.com/michelebardsley

amazon.com/author/michelebardsley

20214407R10100

Made in the USA
Lexington, KY
03 December 2018